# A faint green glow flickered down the basement library corridor...

...a glow that rippled like a reflection on water. All of Tor's irritation at his friends disappeared. His stomach took a swoop like it did the moment when a roller coaster finally drops off the first big hill.

The glow didn't get any stronger, but it started to move closer to them, dancing and swaying back and forth. If the greenish thing kept coming, they were finally going to see the Snow Park Library ghost...

# Also by Bonnie Ramthun

## The Torin Sinclair Mysteries

*The White Gates*
*Roscoe*
*Haunted Waters*

*To Sharon and Walt,*

# HAUNTED
## WATERS

# BONNIE RAMTHUN

*friends forever!*

*enjoy!*

*Brian Ramthun*

*2016*

A Lucky Bat Book

**Haunted Waters**
*A Torin Sinclair Mystery*

Published by Lucky Bat Books
LuckyBatBooks.com
10 9 8 7 6 5 4 3 2 1

ISBN-10: 1-943588-35-X
ISBN-13978-1-943588-35-0

This book is also available in digital formats.

Discover other titles by the author at
http://www.bonnieramthun.com

This novel is dedicated to my son, Jasper Ramthun.
He's always ready for adventure!

# Table of Contents

# Chapter One

## The Library Ghost

The ghost had better show up soon. Tor was sick of being jammed together with his friends in their tiny hiding place in the library basement. His friend Drake had recently decided to adopt the current boy band hair fashion and his wheat-blond bangs hung over his eyes. He also had a thing for horrible sweaters and tonight was one of his worst, a checkered brown sweater with black kittens printed all over the front. The sweater wouldn't be too bad except the kittens all had gigantic eyes. Being stuck for hours in a dark broom closet of the Snow Park Public Library with Drake and his collection of staring cats was getting to be too much.

Tor's other friend Raine didn't have bang problems, but she did have something else that was about to drive Tor completely around the bend. She smelled like garlic. Raine's family were Ute Indians and usually ate Ute meals, sturdy stews and grilled meats and cornbread, but this winter Mrs. Douglas had developed a huge crush on a cable cooking show gourmet whose breathy Italian accent was probably as fake as his dazzling white teeth, and she had been cooking Italian food for months. Raine was so garlicky that if Tor were a vampire, he'd have poofed into dust long before now just from the smell.

"What is that?" Raine whispered. A faint green glow flickered down the basement library corridor, a glow that rippled like a reflection on water. All of Tor's irritation at his friends disappeared. His stomach took a swoop like it did the moment when a roller coaster finally drops off the first big hill.

The glow didn't get any stronger, but it started to move closer to them, dancing and swaying back and forth. If the greenish thing kept coming, they were finally going to see the Snow Park Library ghost.

The town library, built in 1904, looked like an ancient fortress, with battlements and towers at the corners and high narrow windows, as though books and learning needed to be defended with boiling oil and bows and arrows. Old-fashioned lighting and dark oak bookshelves made the library shadowy and mysterious even on the brightest of summer days.

The books had changed over the years, of course, and a whole section of computers, computer games, and movies were now a big part of the main floor. But other than the replacement of the furnace and a new roof, the library was the same building it had been when the *Titanic* sank into the waters of the Atlantic in 1912, the same as it had been when Hitler died in his bunker in 1945, the same when Neil Armstrong stepped on the surface of the moon in 1969. The library held all that history and all those memories within it, in ancient newspapers that Tor had pored over for hours, searching for a reason that a ghost had come to haunt the library basement. He'd found nothing but a lot of history, old architectural drawings, and dust.

Tor's heart rate picked up. The ghost was going to appear at last. And they were there to catch it. The three of them had done all the research they could think of on hauntings. They'd seen a dozen cable television shows about ghost hunters. They'd read lots of books. They'd even watched *Ghostbusters*. *Twice*.

"I'm recording." Drake aimed his phone at the shifting, glimmering light that was still too far away to see clearly. The phone screen was turned off so there was no light to betray them. The closet, their increasingly small and smelly home for the past five nights, was artfully propped open with a mop bucket that looked as though it had rolled the door open a foot or two. In the darkness of the closet Tor tried not to grin, to betray their presence by a flash of white teeth.

Tor's mom, Dr. Sinclair, ran the health clinic in Snow Park and everything exciting that happened in town came through her clinic doors. Tor did his homework there every afternoon after he finished snowboarding on the mountain slopes that surrounded the town. People who came in didn't often notice the quiet figure in the corner of the waiting area, but he noticed them. Tor watched. He listened, and he remembered.

When they'd first moved to Snow Park, Colorado, there were tales of an old curse that was supposed to fall upon the town healer. People believed the curse, and they didn't want to make friends with the new doctor and her son. Tor found himself ignored, or shoved into lockers at school, and he was nearly killed on the slopes while he was learning how to snowboard. Life in Snow Park had been tough those first weeks.

Then he found friends. Drake Wexler, son of a world-famous snowboarder, and his best friend, Raine Douglas, a Ute Indian girl whose ancestor, it turned out, was the one who had cursed the town, decided that they weren't going to let a curse get in the way of making a new friend. Tor found a place in Snow Park.

Now that his mom had run her clinic for two years undisturbed, new rumors started to float about. Tor heard that people started to believe the curse might be broken, and maybe Tor and his friends were the reason.

One day Tor came home after school to find Mrs. Harbin, the town librarian, at his kitchen table with his mom, drinking tea.

"Hello, Tor," Mrs. Harbin said with a smile. Her eyes were red and watery, as if she'd been crying.

"Come have a seat, Tor," his mom said, patting the table. "Mrs. Harbin has come to ask for help."

"From me?" Tor asked, dropping his bag and sitting at the table. Roscoe, his dog, came up and shoved his burly head into Tor's hands. Tor patted Roscoe and tried to keep from showing his confusion.

"Maybe," his mom said.

"It started appearing in January," Mrs. Harbin explained. "We didn't even see it at first. There was just a puddle of water on the floor in the basement shelves. Books were scattered about. The puddle was there every morning, so we searched and searched for a leak. We were frantic to find the source of the water. There's only one thing that's as bad as a fire in a library, and that's a water leak. We found nothing, so we called Mr. Stanley."

"Mr. Stanley?" Tor asked.

"He took over the Mr. Handyman service from Pedro Martinez a few years ago," Mrs. Harbin said.

"Oh yeah, old Mr. Martinez. He wears tinfoil under his hat to keep the aliens away and he's had lunch with Bigfoot—" Tor's grin faded immediately under his mom's measured glance.

"He is an eccentric fellow," Mrs. Harbin said with a touch of frost in her voice. "But he was an excellent handyman. He was ready to retire, so young Gregory Stanley bought the business. He inspected the library roof for us and couldn't find a single leak."

"One night Brenda was closing up and she saw something green and glowing, floating in the basement stacks. It scared her so badly she ran out of the building and fell on the ice and sprained her ankle. The next morning there was the same puddle and a stack of books, right where she'd seen the glow." Mrs. Harbin clutched her empty teacup. "She's so scared she doesn't want to come back. I didn't want to go the police about this. What could they do? And what happens if everyone in town decides the library is haunted? We're on a shoestring of a budget as it is…"

Tor's mom patted Mrs. Harbin's hands. "Don't worry, Rachel. Tor?"

"We'll solve this," Tor said confidently, trying to hide his excitement. A real ghost adventure!

Now, after five long, boring nights of waiting in the closet from closing time until midnight, Tor saw the green glow that frightened Brenda, the glow that sent Mrs. Harbin to his mom's home, turn the corner. Tor couldn't help a tiny hiss escaping from his teeth.

Because there floated a sure-enough, honest-to-gosh *ghost*.

A breath of icy air swept along the polished dark boards of the library basement floor, a breeze that was moist as well as cold. The knuckles of Tor's hand tingled where they pressed against the wood planks. Beside him, Raine quivered. She wasn't afraid; Tor knew her better than that. She was as thrilled as he was. Drake, at his other side, didn't twitch or move but seemed to grow denser, like a cat bunching together before it springs.

The green glowing figure looked like a man, dressed in clothes that were something from the 1800s, when Snow Park was actually a mining town named Coopersville and bank robbers rode horses and stole bags of gold instead of money. The man's pants were shapeless and rough; the shirt looked handmade. The figure wore a big jacket, shapeless and dirty like the pants, and a crumpled old cowboy hat.

More cold air slithered past Tor's hands and touched his legs and feet. His skin pebbled into goose bumps and the hair at the back of his neck prickled. The figure had no feet. The pants ended a few inches above the ground, but there were no boots, no shoes—nothing but blackness. Tor tried to see the figure's face, already knowing what he would see.

The ghost had no face. There was nothing under the cowboy hat but darkness. The hat turned, looking first one way and then another. The ghost floated forward a few steps. The green glow surrounded it as though the light was coming from inside. Tor had seen movie effects like this, but he knew most of that was computer generated, put in by clever artists. They weren't watching a movie right now, or a projection. This was real.

Raine quivered against Tor's shoulder, again, and Drake drew himself up even tighter. They'd been waiting for five long nights now, spending their evening hours hunched in a closet. Tor wanted to capture this thing in the worst way, just to make up for the long miserable hours spent waiting for it. His face felt hot.

The green glowing man floated to the section of books where the puddles had appeared before, and hovered. They watched, and waited, and when the thing took a book from the shelf, Tor saw the green glow surrounding the outline of fingers. He expected skeleton bones, but there was nothing but that unsettling blackness. When the third book came out, that was the signal they'd agreed on.

Raine leaped to her feet and whipped out her phone at the same moment Tor slid to the left, out of the closet, and stumbled over the mop bucket. He took two big steps to keep from falling and then found the cord they'd threaded to the lights. The basement lights flicked on, blindingly bright after the near pitch darkness. Drake sprinted down the aisle next to where the ghost floated, his powerful snowboarder's legs pumping.

"Hey!" Raine yelled. Tor dove and rolled, coming up with his phone in video mode. Raine took pictures, the light flashing. She was dressed in jeans and a long woolen shirt, one moccasined foot braced back, phone held up, teeth bared in a grin.

Tor held his phone up, not taking a breath, and tried to focus on the green ghost.

The thing turned, fleeing, racing away from Torin and Raine. Raine ran fearlessly after it, leaping the puddle of water on the floor, chasing the phantom, her long black braids bouncing behind her. It ran silently before them, faster than anything should have been able to run, and then Drake stepped into the gap at the end of the aisle, grinning, panting. The ghost was trapped.

The figure turned and dove into the wall of books and disappeared. It just vanished. Drake's jaw dropped. Tor, chasing after Raine, got the video on his phone and felt a fierce burst of delight as he saw the glowing green thing go through the solid wall of books. Real, he thought wildly inside his head. *Real!*

Raine stopped, still taking pictures, so she did not see the bookshelf next to her tip toward her. The twelve-foot-high storage shelves, made of old metal, were overloaded with heavy books. The phone dropped from Tor's hands as the top books tumbled from the shelf. Raine realized, too late, that she was about to be buried under books and then crushed by the heavy metal shelves of the bookshelf. The avalanche of books wouldn't kill her, but the bookshelf would. Her body looked slim and fragile, as breakable as a girl made of glass, as the first books fell toward her.

Time slowed to a crawl. Tor saw the arc of descent of the bookshelf draw itself in the air as clean blue glowing lines. The bookshelf would strike the neighboring bookshelf halfway down, and would then send the next bookshelf tumbling down like a domino. If it stopped and didn't slide down flat to the floor, there was a small space, a triangle, between the two bookshelves, where Raine might survive.

Tor bet his life on the triangle. The first book hadn't touched Raine when he was upon her, his arms sweeping around her. He curled up and brought both of them to the floor in the tiny space where his mind had marked out the bright triangle of safety. Raine's knees hit the floor with a terrible crack and a short, sharp cry burst from her. A blow struck him across the shoulders, and then another, like an angry creature pounding him with rough, square fists. Books kept hitting him and dust burst out of them as they struck him. Tor thought he cried out, he couldn't be sure, in the thunder of the books and the groaning of the bookshelf as it gave up hundreds of old books and fell. He heard Drake yell and hoped his friend was clear. Then there was nothing but pain, great oceans of it like surf crashing against every part of him, his arms and back and legs, and something came down like a coffin lid slamming shut and everything went away for a little while.

# Chapter Two

## Book Return

Tor was sleeping. No, he was dreaming. Wait, he was awake, because he could hear Drake.

Drake was shouting his name, and Raine's name, over and over again. Tor couldn't move. A weight pressed down on him, lots of weight. Drake, somewhere, kept calling for him. It was all very annoying.

What, exactly, was going on? Tor's brain just wouldn't sharpen; it wouldn't work right. Had he been buried in an avalanche? He wasn't cold, but he couldn't see and he couldn't move. He opened his eyes, but he couldn't see anything. Something soft lay underneath him, but it didn't feel like a mattress.

"Drake!" someone else shouted, from close by.

"Mr. Stanley!" Drake's voice cracked into childhood again, and Tor heard a whining, panting sound and felt pressure on whatever was covering him. For a moment he couldn't breathe, and the sleepy, uncaring feeling washed away in a panic. He was going to die, suffocate, and he still couldn't move no matter how hard he tried.

9

The snuffling sound came again, and a bark.

"Roscoe," Tor tried to say, but his voice didn't work. Roscoe whined, somewhere close. The pressure eased on his back and legs and Tor would have cried out in relief, except he still couldn't breathe. The air was warm and foul with dust and his own used breath. Where was Drake? And Raine?

"Good boy, Roscoe," Drake said, from somewhere close by. His voice trembled with strain.

"Keep pushing, Drake; put your legs into it," Mr. Stanley's low voice growled. There was a grinding, squealing crash and everything shuddered.

The pressure on Tor's back and legs eased. Roscoe's big paw pulled something aside and sweet, fresh air suddenly surrounded him. Light flooded in. Tor gasped, coughed, tried to move and found out that he could. He was in a pile of books, not an avalanche, and as he blinked the dust out of his blurry eyes he could see Drake and Mr. Stanley on either side of a heavy bookcase. They'd pulled it off and set it upright, and once they had, Roscoe could dig him out from the avalanche of books that had buried him. Him and…

"Raine." Tor rolled off the softness that he'd been lying on and there was Raine, eyes closed, curled up on the cold floor.

"Is she breathing?" Mr. Stanley fell to his knees next to Tor. Tor tried to reach out to Raine but his hand floated in the air, shaking. Meanwhile Mr. Stanley felt her neck for a pulse, and Drake seized Raine's hand.

"Raine, Raine, wake up," Drake whispered hoarsely.

Raine took a deep breath, and opened her eyes. They were fuzzy and far away for a moment, then they brightened.

"You nearly squashed me, you big bear," she said, coughing.

"Sorry." Tor finally managed to reach her hand and patted it clumsily. "Are you okay?"

"I think so," Raine said. Mr. Stanley fell back on his knees and whoofed out a huge sigh. Drake threw himself spread-eagled on the pile of books on the floor and pressed his hand to his chest. Roscoe thought this must be a new game and pounced on Drake, trying to lick his face.

"Get off, get off me," Drake groaned, pushing Roscoe away. "I'm trying to have a heart attack here."

Roscoe padded back to Tor and sat down, panting happily. Tor reached up and felt a big lump on the back of his head. It was the size and shape of a chicken egg. Tor looked at his fingers and saw red. Blood. Well, whatever.

Raine sat up gingerly, feeling her head, then her legs, and hissed with pain when she reached her knees. Tor remembered the sound her knees made when they hit the basement floor and winced.

"Are you okay? Your knees?"

"Bruised. I've had worse," Raine said, then coughed again. Tor did, too. The dust from the fallen books still hung in the air like smoke. It stung Tor's throat and burned in his chest.

"Should we get your mom, Tor?" Mr. Stanley asked anxiously.

"No!" Tor, Drake, and Raine shouted at once.

"Well—" Mr. Stanley looked doubtful.

"Thanks, Mr. Stanley, we're okay," Tor tried to sound confident, and clenched his hand into a fist so the young handyman wouldn't see the blood on it. His mom wouldn't let them continue to ghost hunt if she knew he and Raine had nearly gotten killed. "How did you get here so fast? I thought you were working tonight at the bank."

"I was, but I was keeping an eye out for you, too. It gives me a creepy feeling to be locking you in the library every night. I saw something out the window and there was your big dog, running down the street like he was on a mission. He was flying. I figured I better get here fast."

Tor held out a hand to Roscoe, who pushed his nose into it, his black eyes dancing as if he was having a great time. Then he wrinkled up his nose and sneezed, which made Tor laugh. Roscoe was a stray that he'd adopted last year. He was huge. His golden fur was shaded darker at the tips and created a ruff around his neck, giving him a look like a lion. The markings around his eyes, like an Egyptian painting, made him look wise and knowing.

Tor smoothed Roscoe's head and roughed his ears. If Roscoe hadn't known they were in trouble, Mr. Stanley wouldn't have come along too, and Tor and Raine might have suffocated.

Drake sat up. His boy bangs had lost their fluffiness and looked dirty and clumped. The staring kittens on his sweater all looked dazed too. "Roscoe started digging, and Mr. Stanley and I pulled up the bookshelf, and there you were."

"Thanks, Drake. Thanks, Mr. Stanley." Raine reached out and patted Roscoe. "You too, Roscoe."

"So what happened?" Mr. Stanley asked.

"We saw the ghost," Tor said, and got to his feet. He could feel his muscles starting to throb. He was going to have a big set of bruises all up and down the back of his body.

"No way," Mr. Stanley said, his face falling. He looked scared. "Really?" He looked very young, suddenly, not a grown-up with a job but someone who could be fourteen, like them.

"Really."

"That's—wait." Mr. Stanley looked at the bookshelf, and the piles of books everywhere. "It did that? A *ghost?*"

"You can't tell Mrs. Harbin." Drake got up and picked up some books. "You can't."

"You almost died tonight," Mr. Stanley said seriously, and was suddenly back to looking like an adult. "I have to—"

"Please, don't." Raine scrambled to her feet and picked up some books, wincing as her knees flexed. "We can put all these back. They've all got numbers on them; we can get it done."

Tor and Drake exchanged a look and Tor stifled a groan.

"How can a ghost push over a bookshelf?" Mr. Stanley got to his feet. His dark hair, usually combed neatly, lay over his forehead in untidy curls. He wore a coverall with his name and "Mr. Handyman

Services" embroidered on the back. He looked at the piles of books and dust, and squared his shoulders. He picked up a book, and a breath Tor didn't realize he was holding sighed out of him in relief.

"Thanks, Mr. Stanley." Tor gave Roscoe a last pat and got to his feet. "We could use the help."

As they re-stacked the books, coughing now and then from the dust, they told Mr. Stanley all about the ghost. Roscoe sat and watched them with his dark eyes and looked sad, as though he wished he had hands instead of paws so he could help stack books, too.

"So you might have pictures. And video. Watch your head." Mr. Stanley swung a folding ladder over Drake and set it down. He unfolded it, engaged the safety latches, and climbed up. Raine handed an armful to Tor, who followed Mr. Stanley halfway up the ladder. Tor handed the first books to Mr. Stanley and then reached back to Drake, who handed him more.

"My phone is okay. Tor's isn't." Raine gave him a sympathetic look, and Tor shrugged and tried to look like it didn't matter. He'd saved all his summer earnings to buy a smartphone, which they'd already discovered smashed to bits on the floor. Looking at the remains of the tough little plastic casing of his phone made him think uncomfortably about the fragile curve of Raine's head.

"My phone's okay too, but I don't think I got any video of the ghost on it." Drake stopped for a minute to look at his phone. He shook his head. "Nothing but blurry stuff and then the floor when I dropped it." Drake tucked it away and scooped up a last handful of books. "That's it on this side. Wow, I can't believe we're almost done."

"You three work hard. You could be good handymen." Mr. Stanley grinned down at them and started down the ladder. Tor jumped down and watched him step lightly down.

"Does it pay very well?" Tor asked, as Mr. Stanley folded up the ladder.

"Not too much. But it's all about the uniform," Mr. Stanley said seriously. "It slays the girls. Slays them."

Drake laughed and the handyman grinned. He carried the ladder to the other side of the bookshelf and set it up again. Raine rubbed her forehead, leaving a grimy smear, and picked up a stack of books with a sigh.

"You okay?" Tor took the books from her. She looked as tired as he felt.

"Just a headache. I want to get this done and get home."

"I want to see Raine's pictures," Drake said. "Surely she got some, right?"

"I'd like to see them too." Mr. Stanley reached for the last stack of books. "I didn't get to see the original, like you did."

He put the books away and then they all huddled around Raine's phone. Tor took a look around as Raine pulled up her photo app. The library basement, though very dusty, looked just as it had before. They were all very grimy. The bump on the back of Tor's head throbbed with every beat of his heart.

"There." Raine turned on her phone and focused in on a greenish blob. Tor felt a chill at the back of his neck as the short little hairs back there prickled. The blob was definitely a man, with no feet or hands. A man with no face. Mr. Stanley drew a sharp breath and drew back from the phone as though afraid the ghost would come right out through the little screen.

"We got a picture of it. We got it." Drake smacked one hand into the other fiercely, as though he wanted to pound his fist into the ghost's face.

Raine clicked to the next picture, and the next. "But they're not very good," she said. "They're all a little bit blurry and far away."

"Here's the real problem," Tor said tiredly. Roscoe leaned against him and he patted the dog absently on his enormous head. "We were planning on a total Scooby-Doo here. Capture the guy, rip off his mask, if-it-wasn't-for-those-darned-kids, you know."

Mr. Stanley snorted. Raine looked up from her phone and Drake rubbed his eyes.

"There's no mask to rip off. This is a real ghost."

"You want to give up?" Drake asked angrily.

"No, of course he doesn't." Raine turned off her phone and tucked it in her pocket. "We need to rethink this. Tomorrow. After I get a hot bath and some Ute tea for my bruises. Tor, do you want some, too?"

"I think I've suffered enough for one day." Tor shuddered. Raine's family tea smelled like boiled sweat socks and tasted worse.

"I will walk you all home." Mr. Stanley made this announcement with a lift of his eyebrow, as though daring them to argue.

"Sure," Drake said with a shrug. "But I'm staying at Tor's house right now, and we've got Roscoe. He'd rip any ghost apart like a roasted chicken."

There was a silence in the library. Raine looked at Tor, then Drake, and then Mr. Stanley. All of them stood as though suddenly put into a trance, looking into the distance.

"Mmm, chicken," Tor murmured. Drake and the handyman nodded.

"Oh, please." Raine flipped her braids over her shoulders. "Boys. Okay, Mr. Stanley, you can walk me the whole two blocks home. If it makes you happy."

"It does. If you please."

"Then let's get out of here." Tor picked up a last plastic shard from his phone. Mr. Stanley shut down the lights and they climbed up the stairs and into the main library in the gloom. No one spoke. Tor wasn't even thinking much. He was too tired, and too hungry. Drake opened the doors and a swirl of snow swept in. Big spring snowflakes fell and melted instantly on the sidewalk. Several caught in Raine's black hair and clung like jewels, glittering in the light from the street lamps.

Tor looked down the street at Snow Park, his home, nestled at the base of three huge mountains. Snow Park was a picture-perfect little Alpine village that drew winter skiers and snowboarders by the thousands. Antique lamps lined the main streets where a multitude of shops tempted the pocketbooks of people who'd finished skiing for the day. There were restaurants, spas, rental shops, and hotels in Snow Park, a cozy resort that Tor thought was the most perfect place to live, ever.

Now everything was dark and silent, all the shops closed, all the restaurants dark. Snowflakes fell from a night sky that had the luminous glow of heavy snow to come.

Raine lived right on Main Street, in a big apartment above the ski and snowboard rental shop that her parents owned. Tor could see where she lived from the library steps, and he watched Mr. Stanley and Raine walk down the street together as Drake and Roscoe stood with him.

Drake made no attempt to head toward Tor's house, and neither did Tor. They watched Raine and Mr. Stanley get smaller and smaller as the snowflakes fell faster. The snow melted on the back of Tor's neck and made his skull lump sting, and he was so hungry he couldn't even think straight, but he waited until he saw Raine disappear into her family's door.

Mr. Stanley turned and gave them a wave, then headed down the street. Tor couldn't see his smile from that far away, but he knew the man was smiling.

"He knows we don't trust him." Tor shook snow from his shoulders and started walking.

"He knows we watch out for Raine." Drake followed him.

Tor thought of grilled cheese on toast, of a bowl of Cheerios so big he could take a lap in it like a swimming pool, of leftover lasagna heated up and bubbling—

"Hey, Drake. Mom made lasagna yesterday. I think there's some leftover—"

Drake seized the back of his jacket and yanked him sideways so he stumbled, and then took off in a sprint. Drake had nearly three seconds' head start before Tor caught up and they raced, trying not to make any sound, laughing, for Tor's door. Roscoe galloped with them, tongue hanging out, panting happily.

Later, his belly full of hot food, Tor scrambled into bed. Drake had slept on a spare mattress for a while, but then Tor's mom had bought bunk beds for them. Drake didn't live with them all the time, but when his famous dad was out of town or when he was having one of his big house parties, Drake ended up at the Sinclairs' house. Drake was already asleep in the upper bunk, snoring slightly, his annoying hair back into perfect boy band fluffiness.

Roscoe stood in the doorway. Tor patted his hand on the bed. Roscoe usually slept at the end of the bed, snoring like Drake, occasionally snorting and twitching and having bad dreams just like a human being. Tor frowned. Roscoe didn't trot in and jump on the bed. Instead, his dog stood in the doorway and didn't come in. His tail wasn't wagging, either.

"What's up, boy?"

Roscoe turned away and padded down the hall. Tor groaned and got out of bed. He turned to look at Drake but his friend was out, solidly asleep.

Roscoe stood at the back door as though he wanted to go out into the yard.

"Oh, Roscoe, why now?" Tor grumbled. He opened the door and folded his arms against the swirling snowflakes that were finally started to stick. The ground was covered in white. Roscoe stood in the doorway and did not go into the yard.

"What is—" Tor saw what Roscoe was staring at and his breath stopped in his throat as though a hand had closed around it. He couldn't breathe.

Theirs was the last house on the block. Behind them stretched an alpine meadow, and then the mountainside swept steeply up, covered in pine trees and snow.

Deep in the pines stood a green glowing figure. Watching him.

# Chapter Three

## Veggie Girl

"**N**o way." Raine clutched her books to her chest.

"Way. It was watching me." Tor leaned close so only Raine could hear him. Students jostled him on either side, struggling to get books into or out of their lockers. Raine grabbed her lunch bag from her locker and slammed it shut, and they worked their way out of the crowd. Drake arrived moments later, out of breath, his books under his arm. Today's sweater was an old favorite, a shaggy brown thing that looked like it was made out of Bigfoot hair.

"I'm starved," he announced. Everyone wore snow boots, and the shuffling sound of hundreds of boots against the grimy floor, together with the noise of everyone talking at once, made conversation impossible.

"What do you think this means?" Raine asked when they were in the lunchroom and it was a bit more quiet. She stood with them in the lunch line, though she didn't pick up a tray. She always brought her own lunch. Tor often thought he should pack his lunch, like Raine. The cafeteria food of Snow Park Middle/High School was the stuff of student legend—and not in a good way. Somehow the thought of packing his own lunch always occurred to him after he was already starving and already in line. He looked at the tray of cooked spinach in front of him and grimly held out his plate. It was food, and he was hungry.

"Maybe it's going to haunt Tor now." Drake sounded matter-of-fact as he held out his tray for spinach but Tor felt a chill just the same. Could the ghost decide to come after him, just like that? Why? He held out his plate to the next cafeteria lady and she gave him a tiny helping of crispy chicken nuggets. The macaroni and cheese came out of her other spoon with a gluey sound and plopped onto his plate.

"Thank you." Tor sighed and moved to the checkout lane, digging his school ID out of his pants. Drake ran his card through the reader and tucked it back into his pocket, balancing his tray on one hand. He looked around the cafeteria.

"Well that doesn't make much—oh, Drake. No," Raine protested, but Drake was already heading for Veggie Girl's table. "We can't talk there!"

"We'll talk later." Drake tossed his hair back in his boy band way that made Tor want to throttle him. Raine sighed and followed. Tor did too, noticing the way Drake gathered all eyes to him as he sauntered to Veggie Girl's table. The most popular girl in their class, Caroline, ran a hand down her long blonde hair and laughed loudly just as Drake walked by. He didn't glance her way, and Tor suppressed a smirk as she threw a smoldering, angry glance at Veggie Girl.

Caroline and her friends didn't know why handsome Drake Wexler was so taken with the very odd Veggie Girl. Tor did, though, and he approved.

"Gemma. Tanya. Marie." Drake sat at the table and smiled brilliantly at the three girls sitting across from him. If he'd smiled at Caroline and the other cheerleaders that way, they would have exploded into giggles of excitement. These three glowered at him.

"Drake. Tor. Raine." Gemma drawled Raine's name. Raine looked back at her with no expression and sat down. Gemma was a thin girl, with shoulder-length blonde hair held back by barrettes. She had very pale, freckled skin. Her eyes were squinched together in disapproval behind her glasses.

"Chicken nuggets today." Drake looked from Gemma to Tanya and Marie. Tanya wore an expression of faint disgust, but Tor noticed the girls had managed to save room at their table for Drake and his friends.

"These are terrible for you." Gemma pushed a napkin piled high with chicken nuggets toward Drake and Tor, the combined portions of the three girls. "They're meat. Meat is bad for you, and then to add processing, white flour, sodium, it's just terrible."

"Terribly delicious." Drake munched one up and gave the girls a sunny smile. "Thanks."

"Thanks," Tor said too, although he didn't have to say anything at all for the notice that they gave him. The addition of the three girl's nuggets to their own meant that Tor and Drake actually got a filling lunch.

Raine opened her bag and took out her lunch. She took a big, obvious bite of a venison and lettuce sandwich, chewed, and looked at Gemma, who stared back at her. Gemma's eyes squinched almost shut in disapproval.

"Our whole ecosystem is out of balance," Gemma said to no one in particular. "We need to be in harmony, not in this terrible cycle of using. Before we know it, we'll be out of resources. Out of clean water, and air, and fresh food. Out of time."

Drake wolfed his chicken nuggets and nodded at Gemma as though she were spouting the greatest wisdom in the world. Tor ate his lunch quickly. He liked the extra food but he wished he could talk to Raine about last night.

"You okay, Tor?" For a moment Tor couldn't figure out who was speaking to him, and then he realized it was Gemma. She wasn't using her save-the-planet voice and sounded completely different, almost like a normal girl.

"Late night last night." Tor said after a moment, after struggling with a mouthful of chicken nuggets and surprise at actually being addressed by Veggie Girl. She never spoke to him. He didn't know she even knew his name. "Uh, studying."

"There's something going on," Gemma said in a low voice. She looked at her friends, then at Drake and Raine, and finally at Tor, and sighed in exasperation. "I know I always say that, but it's true. There's something *wrong* in the forests around Snow Park."

Tor opened his mouth, curious to ask Gemma some questions. Could she, too, be haunted by a green glowing figure? Had she seen it? Before he could speak, Raine kicked him hard in the shins.

"Hey!"

"Look." Raine was staring at the entrance to the lunchroom. Tor turned to see a group of students walk into the room. In the lead was a familiar face to everyone in school, wearing a big grin and a bright yellow jacket. David Malone. Behind him swaggered Max Nye, his best friend, in the same bright yellow.

Tor felt his stomach drop. The matching jackets could mean only one thing.

"The snowboarding team is back in business!" David Malone yelled and pumped his fists, and all the students in the lunchroom applauded and cheered wildly. Max Nye made a bodybuilder move to show off his arms.

"Oh, great." Tor rubbed his hand through his hair and winced in pain as he touched the tender lump at the back of his head.

"How did they get reinstated?" Raine asked. "After only a year? How?"

"His dad's the mayor," Drake said, popping the last of the chicken nuggets into his mouth and speaking through a mouthful of food. "One year is a minimum time for a team to sit on the bench if they're caught cheating."

"Or killing people," Tor said. Tanya let out a little squeak and Gemma put her head close to the other girl's and started whispering rapidly. Tor saw heads turning his way, whispered conversations, and felt a terrible sensation in his stomach. Was it all going to happen all over again? Being knocked into lockers, shoved around, tripped, kicked?

"Smile. Right now," Raine hissed. "Then give a little wave."

"Why?"

"Just do it." Raine grinned at the lunchroom and Tor did the same. Drake also gave a wave, and tossed his hair back from his eyes. Tor felt the focus of hundreds of eyes on him, and then students turned away and started chattering to each other again. In a few minutes the snowboarders had finished their victory lap and sat down in the lunchroom. With Caroline, Tor noticed, the pretty cheerleader. Of course.

"What was that all about?" Tor asked Raine. "Why did you have me wave at them?"

"You weren't the bad guy, Tor; the guy who made them cheat was the bad guy. If you act like you're the one who got the team kicked off competition for a year, everyone is going to believe it too."

"She's right. Tor, you *caught* the bad guy." Drake reminded him. "Well, with our help of course." He got up from the table, used a napkin to wipe his mouth, and tossed the used napkin on his tray. He picked it up and gave Veggie Girl and her friends a sunny grin. "Good day, ladies. Save us a seat next time."

"Sure, Drake," Tanya said, blushing fiercely and trying to look as if she didn't care a bit all at the same time. Gemma ignored him, staring into space, lost in thought. Something about her worried expression caught at Tor.

"Let's go, Tor." Raine nudged his elbow, and he scrambled to his feet.

When they left the lunchroom, Tor spotted Mr. Ewald standing against the wall, looking out of place and uncomfortable. Mr. Ewald had an egg-shaped body and thinning hair on his large, round head. He reminded Tor of Humpty Dumpty. He was a great math teacher, though, and Tor liked being in his class. Mr. Ewald knew how to explain math in a way that made sense.

"Hi, Mr. Ewald," they chorused as they left the room. Tor turned to head toward Raine's locker. Mr. Ewald stepped away from the wall and put up a hand.

"Excuse me. Tor, may I have a minute?"

Tor exchanged surprised looks with Drake and Raine, then nodded. "See you after school," he called.

"Snow Eagle chair lift, three o'clock," Drake called back, and he and Raine headed down the hall. Tor grinned. The slopes were going to be spectacular today after the big snowstorm last night.

"What's up, Mr. Ewald?"

"This isn't about math class. You're doing quite well." Mr. Ewald cleared his throat.

"Thanks." Tor put his hands in his pockets and waited.

"I—I'm the new coach of the snowboarding team. I know, I know. I don't snowboard. But the school board felt that someone who wasn't so—involved—with competition and winning would be a good way to get the snowboarding team started again. We'll be training through the summer and getting ready for fall competitions." Mr. Ewald took a tissue out of his pocket and dabbed at his forehead. Behind Tor, students came out of the lunchroom and gave them curious looks. Mr. Ewald tilted his head and Tor walked with him down the hall.

"I'm real glad, Mr. Ewald. I think you'll be a great coach." Tor wasn't sure what Mr. Ewald wanted him to say. Raine was right; Tor wasn't the reason the snowboarding team had been suspended. They had cheated and Tor had caught them. So—

"I want you to try out for the team." Mr. Ewald dabbed at his forehead again. Tor felt his jaw drop and he came to a stop in the hallway.

"What?"

"I want you to try out for the snowboarding team. You're only a freshman but you're fast. You'll be a terrific boarder cross competitor."

For a moment Tor couldn't understand what Mr. Ewald was saying, as though he was speaking a foreign language. Then Tor realized what the teacher meant. He could be in snowboarding competitions. Tor loved to go fast on his snowboard. The speed, the power of slamming a snowboard down a hill in an elbow-to-elbow race to the finish line, floating over jumps and nearly flying, all of that to the roar and the cheers of the crowd. It would be unbelievable. It would be amazing. It would be—

"Ridiculous."

"What? No, not for a minute—"

"I'm a freshman, Mr. Ewald. I couldn't win a spot on the team, and you know it."

"Not yet, but next year," Mr. Ewald said stubbornly. "You could be a team manager. Besides, it would send—it would send the right message."

"Like a mascot, or something? I caught the last team cheating so now I'm your charm to tell everyone the team is honest now?"

"Consider it a compliment." Mr. Ewald took off his glasses and polished them. "I'm afraid I was appealing to your emotion and I'm never good at that. Rationally, then, logically, it would reassure the school district to have the boy who got the team suspended—"

"I believe they did that to themselves," Tor said coldly.

"Yes, er. Yes. At any rate, consider my offer. Don't say no right now, please. Time to get to class. Thanks for talking to me, Tor."

The bell rang and Mr. Ewald held out a tardy pass, already pre-signed. Tor took it and went to his class on automatic pilot, barely thinking about where he was or what he was doing.

The snowboarding team. He'd been offered a place on the snowboarding team.

# Chapter Four

## Out of Bounds

"What was that all about?" Drake asked, as Tor snapped his boot into his snowboard and settled his helmet on this head. Tor slid to the chairlift with Raine and Drake and hopped on. This late in the season and this late in the day there were no lift lines to speak of. The only other people in the chair line were townies like them, getting a last few runs in for the day. The air was cold and the skies were heavy, promising more spring snow.

As the lift hauled them toward the top of the mountain, Tor adjusted his gloves and cleared his throat.

"Mr. Ewald wanted me to help with the snowboarding team. Be a junior manager or something."

Drake sneered. "Right, junior manager. That means you get to carry around dirty uniforms and fetch them water. I'd rather die."

"Me, too," Tor said, and they bumped gloved fists together.

Raine shook her head. "They want cover, right? They want to reassure the district that Snow Park is honorable." Raine smoothed her gloves, opening and closing her fingers to get them just right.

Tor leaned back in the chairlift as pine trees zoomed underneath their dangling feet. Floating up the mountain in a chairlift was the closest thing to a magic carpet ride. The last thing he wanted was to see the Snow Park snowboarding team in their yellow jackets on the mountain again. David Malone and Max Nye were bullies, and they were on the team. As seniors, they were now team leaders. Terrific.

"We need otter time." Drake announced. "We can go see them. Like a spiritual journey or something."

"What?" Raine's mouth twitched into a grin. "A spiritual journey? Who are you and what did you do with Drake?"

"Hey now, don't be a hater. We need otter time. Whenever we see them, we figure out the right thing to do." Drake shrugged. "Right?"

"Ha! You're right. I'm in." Raine settled her helmet on her head and clicked the strap shut.

"Me, too." Tor got ready for the dismount from the chairlift. A secret snowboarding path on the upper mountain led out of bounds and onto Raine's family land. Deep within the mountain was a hidden valley where a family of otters lived and played, unseen by any eyes but theirs.

The valley was magic. Tor felt better when he visited, even though the way back meant a long trip on their snowboards down to the highway and a mile-long hike back to town. Being with the otters, watching them in their secret valley, made everything better. Choices, decisions, maybe even a way out of Tor's problems, they would all become manageable.

He hopped off the chairlift in the dismount area and his board came alive under his feet. He sped over to the second chairlift that would take them up to the top of Snow Park mountain, spats of snowflakes stinging his cheeks with cold. Drake and Raine followed, fresh snow flying from their boards. They were the last ones to ride the upper lift for the day. The chairlift operator put the closed sign up as they swept up and out into the high mountain air. Once they hopped off, it was a quick, exhilarating rush down fresh spring snow to the break in the trees that led to their secret path.

Drake took a look around and carved into the trees first, and Raine disappeared after him. Tor took a last quick glance. No one was near. He shot into the darkness of the pines.

"Yeah!" Drake pumped his fist and Tor laughed out loud. Out of bounds and in the trees, the snow was thick and deep, a perfect spring snow that made their boards float as though they were flying. Going out of bounds was very dangerous but their path wasn't. They all knew this secret way by heart. It led down through a slope of thick pines, across a meadow, down another slope and then finally to the lip of a drop-off that led to their secret valley.

The otter's secret valley, Tor reminded himself. Raine would smack him on the head if he called the valley "theirs." His head lump from last night's adventure in the library gave a twinge at the thought.

Drake stopped, sat down in the snow, and unbuckled from his snowboard. Raine slid up next to him and did the same. Tor, last in line, sat to Raine's right and unbuckled too. They sat on their boards and dangled their feet over the edge and observed the valley below them. In summertime, the valley was noisy with rushing creeks and little water-falls, all draining into the larger creek below. Now, in springtime, the area was covered with snow and only the center of the creek was open, dark and shiny and rippling with icy water. Pine trees towered on all sides of the valley, thick and green and frosted with snow.

Tor could see tracks of otters at play but he couldn't see any of the little animals right now. The otters liked to slide in the snow like kids, and after a while wore a groove like a luge. They'd throw themselves into the slippery chute and zoom down to splash into the water. It was late in the day and Tor and his friends couldn't stay long. Snow lay over everything, heavy and deep, and it was so quiet Tor could hear the beating of his heart. And an odd sort of rumbling sound.

The rumbling didn't sound like Drake's stomach, and not like a plane engine, the only other noise that interrupted their valley before spring thaw turned it into a rushing world of melting water and fast, cold little creeks.

"What's that sound?" Tor asked. Raine tilted her head, listening, and then the color drained out of her face like milk pouring from a glass. Her face became so pale Tor could see the veins in her cheeks and under her eyes.

"Raine?"

Raine looked around oddly, as though her neck was very stiff, first left and then right. Tor saw horror touch her eyes as she looked beyond him. Tor turned and his stomach dropped right into his feet.

A huge mountain lion sat on a rock ledge less than twenty feet from them. It glared at them with glowing green eyes, slit-pupiled, and the rumbling in its chest became a snarl.

Tor shifted left, grabbed his snowboard, and stood up. The mountain lion wrinkled its snout to reveal gigantic yellow teeth. It roared and bunched itself together exactly like a housecat getting ready to leap on something. A moment later, lashing its tail, it leaped right at Tor.

Tor's snowboard slid in slow motion in front of him as the mountain lion grew larger. Someone screamed and Tor wasn't sure if it was the lion or Raine. Or him. The lion floated through the air, getting bigger and bigger, teeth flashing, claws extended, and the board came between Tor and the mountain lion at the last possible moment.

The impact drove all the breath from Tor and he was thrown backward into the snow, holding his snowboard in front of him. The world was a blur of fur and thrashing as the lion screamed and clawed at the snowboard. Tor dimly thought that he was an idiot to hope a half inch of plastic with a wood core would shield him from two hundred pounds of angry cat. It would be funny if he wasn't the one under the board, and if he could breathe. The cat yowled as something thudded into it and he heard other screaming, but it wasn't him. Any second, the lion was going to hook him out from under the board like a cat snatching a treat. He tried to remember what he'd been taught about mountain lion attacks.

"Never give up fighting a mountain lion," Raine's dad had explained last winter, his odd yellow eyes intent on the three of them as they sat around a mountain campfire. Tor and Drake had fathers, but neither one took them camping like Mr. Douglas did, or taught them how to make fires in snowy woods or how to find water, or taught them what to do if a mountain lion attacked.

"Lions are predators. If predators are injured they don't survive. A deer doesn't fight back, so if you fight hard enough the mountain lion will break off the attack and run off. A man fought off a lion a few years ago with a tiny pocketknife." Mr. Douglas made a stabbing gesture with his fist.

"Did he kill it?" Drake asked.

"No. He shoved the penknife into the mountain lion's ear while the cat was chewing on his head. He had hundreds of stitches, but he survived."

"Oh." Tor and Drake exchanged glances, the equivalent of saying "Yikes!"

"So, what do you do if you see a mountain lion?" Mr. Douglas asked.

"Look as large as possible. Bring your coat up over your head, try to look big," Drake said promptly.

"Make noise." Raine offered.

"Throw things, like pine cones. Scare it off," Tor said.

"Good." Mr. Douglas nodded at them.

Tor struggled under the board and the weight of the big cat, thinking that he tried the first part but he couldn't get his board up in time. The whole making-noise part wouldn't work because he couldn't breathe, and the pine cone part was pretty funny, considering. All his snowboarding muscles, all his strength, meant nothing. He couldn't move. An enormous yellow claw flexed around the edge of the board and came within an eyelash of slicing into Tor's gloved hand. He thrashed, pushed with all his might, and suddenly the mountain lion rolled off him.

Breathing hard, dizzy, Tor stood up and yanked his board with him. He blinked to clear his eyes. The mountain lion lay in the snow at his feet.

It didn't get up. It just lay there, panting, paws twitching, its tail flicking weakly.

"What did you do?" Tor gasped. Raine held her board in her hands, her eyes wide and wild.

"We whacked it with our boards," Raine gasped.

"Did we kill it?" Drake held his snowboard like a club over his shoulder, ready to hit the lion again.

Tor's vision cleared as his deep breaths started to get more oxygen into his starved body. At the end of every deep breath Raine made a little sobbing sound. Drake heaved big breaths in and out too. Before them, the enormous yellow lion snarled and the tip of its long tail twitched again, but it didn't lift its head. Tor could smell the lion, a wild musk that caught in his nose and made him think of the zoo. The fur of the cat was deep and thick and the markings around its eyes and nose reminded Tor of Roscoe. The cat blinked slowly once more and then its eyes slipped shut. The black tip of its tail shuddered, and the cat lay still.

"Oh, no." Raine fell to her knees in the snow. Her snowboard fell behind her.

Tor found himself on his knees next to Raine. Hesitating, she reached and touched the lion's fur. There was no reaction. Tor knew there wouldn't be. The mountain lion was dead. He touched the animal's paw, thick and plush, feeling the hardness of the enormous claws within. It wasn't as big as he thought a mountain lion was supposed to be. It wasn't much bigger than a medium-sized dog.

"Did we kill it?" Drake asked. He let his snowboard sag off his shoulder until it rested in the snow. "We couldn't have killed it. I just wanted to drive it off."

"I don't think we killed it." Raine touched the lion's side. "Look at its ribs. It was starving. And look, the fur is all patchy. I think it was sick."

Tor thought of Gemma, their Veggie Girl with her barrettes and her serious look and her claim that there was something wrong in the forests around Snow Park. The ghost, glowing green in the forest behind his house—was that another part of the something wrong going on? Tor looked at the paw of the lion and saw speckles of blood. The lion must have been injured before it attacked him. An instant later, another drop fell and made a bright red coin in the snow. Then another.

Tor realized suddenly that the lion wasn't bleeding. He was.

# Chapter Five

## The Travois in the Woods

"Tor." Drake snatched Tor's glove and pulled back the sleeve of his jacket. A cut ran across his wrist. It welled with blood and dripped.

"I didn't even feel it." Tor still couldn't feel it. There was no pain at all, though as he looked at the slice he could see that it was deep. He was going to need stitches.

"It's the cold." Raine sat down on her board and unzipped her jacket. She pulled out a soft leather bag with First Aid written on the side in her dad's neat penmanship. "Once you get inside, that's going to bleed like crazy. Sting, too. Here." Raine pulled out a roll of gauze and wrapped it around his wrist. The gauze immediately soaked through with red. Raine frowned and kept winding until the roll was gone.

"Tor, it cut you. That's bad." Drake looked at the body of the mountain lion and he and Raine exchanged glances.

"We have rabies in California, too, guys." Tor pulled his sleeve back down over the cut. He felt better when he couldn't see it. "I don't think he was rabid. He didn't act like a rabid animal."

"He was dying already when he jumped on you, Tor. We don't know what was wrong with him." Raine stuffed the first aid kit back in her coat and pulled her gloves back on.

The silence surrounded them, deep and listening. In the valley below, Tor could see no sign of the otters. Snowflakes started to fall from the gray sky. He felt shivery and his head hurt. He forced the feeling deep inside himself and made it go away. They were miles from town. He had to hold it together.

"I think we have to take it with us." Drake reached out as though he was going to touch the lion and then pulled back. "If it's rabid."

"It's not rabid." Tor's wrist gave a twinge and he tried not to wince.

"But we need to take it anyway." Raine nodded. "They need to run tests to see what happened to it."

"How are we going to bring it with us?" Drake asked.

"We'll make a travois and pull him behind us. It's like a sled made out of pine branches. He's not too big. We'll snowboard out." Raine got to her feet and clapped her gloves together.

Drake got up, picked up his snowboard and set it edge-first into the snow. "That'll work."

Raine helped Drake pull a branch down from a pine tree, breaking it from the trunk. Tor took the branch and laid it next to the lion, working one-handed. He held his hurt hand next to his body. Two or three more branches and they had a makeshift sled. Drake used the leash from his snowboard to bind the branches together. Raine used her leash to make a carrying strap. Drake and Raines crouched down to the mountain lion and rolled it onto the branches. Raine carefully curled up the long tail and laid it along the body. It was so long that she tucked the black-tipped end under his paws. She crouched for a moment, touching the fur over the animal's ribs.

"He's so thin." She stood up, and put her mittened hands on her hips. "He's really thin."

Tor suddenly felt watched. His neck prickled and his stomach shrank into a ball of ice as he whipped his head around. There was no one behind them. He peered into the trees upslope, where they'd snow-boarded in and where their tracks still showed among the dark pine trees. Nothing.

"What's up?" Drake turned to look, too. "What did you see?"

"Nothing." Tor still felt it, though, the weight of someone or some-thing watching them. "I didn't see anything. I just feel watched. All of a sudden."

"I feel it too." Raine adjusted the strap that held the mountain lion to the travois and stood up. She clicked her snowboard helmet strap under her chin. "Time to go."

"Tor, you first. Raine and I will pull the traviois." Drake adjusted his jacket and picked up the snowboard leash that was wrapped around the end of the pine-branch travois.

"I should—"

"You got hit twice in two days. You need to be in front." Raine shrugged her shoulders. "Just in case you fall down, you waster."

"And you start foaming at the mouth. And then you turn into a were-cougar." Drake grinned. "We won't kill you, though. We'll keep you in a cage and feed you prairie dogs."

"And mice," Raine said, and giggled. Tor forced a laugh, because he couldn't say what was on his mind. That Raine was a girl. Even though she was a Ute warrior who could build a fire in five minutes with one match and ride a snowboard like a pro, she was a girl, and he was bigger and stronger and should be the one to pull the travois with Drake. Tor thought that if he dared say that to Raine right now, she'd kick his butt.

"Okay, I'll go first." Tor followed the blazes that the three of them had marked on the trees. The route wasn't too difficult but it led through some dense brush and thick trees. Eventually, when Tor's head seemed to have swollen and was knocking into his helmet with every heartbeat, he spotted the dark ribbon of the highway.

Behind him, Drake panted evenly but hoarsely. Luckily the way was downhill, but the pine branches didn't slide as easily in the snow as their slick snowboards did.

"Almost there," Raine gasped. Tor slid the last hundred feet to the road and crouched, watching. A car drove by fast, lights blazing. The afternoon was turning quickly into night.

"Coast is clear!" He unstrapped from his board and tossed it over the barbed wire that was printed with "Danger!" signs every few feet. Raine joined him and they held up the wire. Drake pulled the mountain lion under. In a moment they were on the legal side of the fence.

Raine fumbled inside her jacket and produced her cell phone. "Mom? It's Raine. We had a problem—yeah, we're okay, we're all okay. Tor needs some stitches maybe—"

"Don't say that!" Drake hissed.

"No, no, we're on the highway by Borsh Mountain. I'll explain later. Can you call Mr. Barton and ask him to bring his truck?"

Tor heard a short, sharp sentence, and the disconnect of the call.

"Let's rest," Raine sighed, putting her cell phone back in her jacket and zipping it closed. "Mom's calling Mr. Barton. He'll give us a ride. She'll call your mom, too, Tor."

"Who's Mr. Barton?" Tor had heard the name but he didn't know where.

"He's the Division of Wildlife Warden for the county," Drake explained. "He's the one that'll take the mountain lion and get it tested for rabies. I think so, anyway."

"We brought him a hurt owl when we were ten." Raine set her board in the snow and clapped her hands together to keep them warm. "Remember, Drake? It was like a big fluffy football. A car hit and it couldn't fly, but it sure tried to peck us to death when we picked it up."

"I wanted to keep it. But Mr. Barton said that owls don't make good pets, even if you read about them in books and stuff. So he fixed it up and fed it mice until it got better." Drake set his board next to Raine's and Tor did the same. Behind them, the mountain lion slowly disappeared under a layer of snow. They were getting covered, too. Raine's snowboard helmet was completely white.

"Mr. Barton let us see it fly away, the day he released it. He's cool."
Raine peered down the road and nodded in satisfaction. "Here he comes."

A few moments later an enormous, pale tan truck pulled over next
to them. The truck was a super cab so it had enough room for all of
them. Tor spotted a round sticker on the side door. The man inside
wasn't wearing a uniform and he didn't look like a cop. He looked like
a lumberjack. He wore a red flannel shirt and he had thick, wiry blond
hair, bright blue eyes, a reddish beard, and big white teeth.

"What's up, kids?" His voice was cheerful and really loud.

"We got attacked by a mountain lion," Raine said. "It jumped us
and then just fell over and died. Tor got cut."

The smile disappeared instantly. Mr. Barton turned on the emergency blinkers on his truck and got out. He loomed over them.

"You all right, son?" A hand as big as a baseball mitt came down on
Tor's shoulder.

"I'm fine. We brought the lion with us." Tor gestured behind him,
to the travois lying on the snow. Inside the truck, a face suddenly
appeared in the window, eyes wide and shocked. The last person Tor
would have expected to see was looking at him.

Veggie Girl. She stared at the lion with her hands held to her mouth.
Tor felt a sudden kinship with her. She looked as shocked as he'd felt
when the mountain lion had died.

"We went a little bit out of bounds." Raine shuffled from one boot
to the other.

"Yeah. We were resting, and it jumped on us. Er, on Tor." Drake
pounded his mittens together. Tor didn't feel cold at all, but Drake and
Raine looked frozen. Raine's nose was bright red.

"Then it just fell into the snow and died," Tor added.

"Okay. Gemmie, get in the back with Tor and Raine. Drake, can
you help me get this animal into the truck?"

"Sure, sir," Drake said. Tor took a breath to protest but Raine tapped
his arm.

"You're bleeding."

She was right. His mitten was soaked and dark with blood. Mr. Barton opened the door to the truck and Gemma scrambled into the back. Raine hopped in without another word. Tor followed, feeling as though he should be helping Drake and Mr. Barton anyway.

The inside was warm and dry and felt wonderful. Gemma scooted over and made room for them, her eyes wide and shocked as she saw Tor's mitten.

"I didn't know you were the warden's daughter," Tor said.

"Sure. Always have been. Is that?" Gemma pointed. She wasn't wearing gloves and her hands looked pale and cold.

"Yeah, it got me. But it doesn't hurt."

"Yet," Raine said grimly. The truck rocked back and forth as Mr. Barton and Drake put the big body of the cat into the back. Tor saw his snowboard and Raine's in Mr. Barton's big grip, and winced as he heard them rattle into the back, next to the mountain lion. Well, he was going to have to rewax his board anyway. If there were marks on the front, though, he'd leave them there, because it would be really kicking to have mountain lion scratches on his board.

Mr. Barton opened the door and got in one side, and Drake opened the door and got in the other. In the few minutes that Mr. Barton had been outside, the snow had covered his head in white, like a frosted cupcake. He shook his head and wiped the snow from his shoulders, then turned around to speak to Tor and Raine.

"I'll drop you off at your folks', Raine. Then your house, Tor. Your mom said to take you there instead of the clinic. Drake?"

"Tor's house."

"Right." Mr. Barton put the truck into gear and they pulled out onto the highway. Tor looked back to see the little pile of branches of the travois lying scattered in the snow. Gemma twisted around too, to look into the bed of the truck where the mountain lion lay.

"We didn't kill it," Tor said in a low voice, as they both stared at the big cat. It seemed so undignified so see it lying in the bed of a pickup truck with snowboards stacked up next to it.

"I know you didn't," Gemma said back to him in an equally low voice. "There's something wrong in the woods. Something really wrong. I know about—"

"What?" Tor asked.

Gemma glanced at the back of Raine's head and pressed her lips together and frowned. "Nothing."

# Chapter Six

## Stitches in the Kitchen

**M**r. Barton turned on the windshield wipers and the blades swept aside the heavy, wet snow and flicked them into the darkness behind the truck. Tor could see the lights of the Conoco station at the edge of town, where they usually stopped for a soda after hiking or snowboarding. They were almost home.

"Mr. Barton, are you going to do a necropsy?" Raine asked. "Because if you are, do you think we could see it?"

"You want to see the necropsy?" Mr. Barton asked in surprise. "Of course I'm doing one; I'm going to have to—"

"What's a necropsy?" Drake asked.

"An autopsy on an animal," Tor responded. "Right?"

"That's right." Mr. Barton rumbled down Main Street and pulled up at Raine's place with a wet crunch of tires in the snow. "If you'd like, you can watch. I'll do a complete examination of the lion to see how it died, what diseases it might have, and what it's been eating."

"And a rabies test too, right?" Drake asked.

43

"Right. But the information we gather will tell us a lot about the health of the forest and the entire ecology of the area."

Tor felt something grip his thigh and looked down to see Gemma's pale hand on his leg, squeezing. She narrowed her eyes at him as though she was trying to tell him something without saying anything aloud. He felt completely confused and she saw that in his face, because she shook her head slightly and moved her hand away. She folded her arms, frowning. In the meantime Mr. Barton kept talking.

"I'll send samples of the brain tissue to a laboratory and we'll know in a day or so if it was rabid. I'm afraid you'll have to have rabies shots anyway, Tor. Your mom will talk to you about that."

"It didn't bite him, though; he got cut by a claw. Don't you have to be bitten to get rabies?" Drake took his helmet off and rubbed his hands through his hair. Tor wanted to take his own helmet off, but he didn't want to move his wrist. His wrist burned like as if it were on fire, and with every beat of his heart the burning got worse. Gemma stared out the window. She was confusing and his wrist wouldn't stop throbbing.

"We won't take the chance with rabies. It's too dangerous, so Tor will have the shots and he'll be okay no matter what." Mr. Barton got out of the truck and helped Raine get her snowboard from the back. Raine gave a quick wave, put her snowboard under her arm, and disappeared into her apartment.

"Let's get you home, boys." Mr. Barton engaged the clutch and they rumbled up the street. The truck bounced over a rut in the road and Tor bit down on a yelp. Roscoe stood at the gate as they drove up, his enormous paws on the top and half his body looming all the way over it. He gave an anxious bark as Mr. Barton opened the door to the truck, and then he did a curious thing. He put his nose into the air and sniffed, hard. Then the big dog sneezed, and he sniffed again. Roscoe's fur began to rise all over his body. In seconds his dog was the size of a bear, and Roscoe's anxious bark turned into a rippling snarl. He dropped back from the gate and backed up several steps, his shoulders hunching up and his back paws digging into the snow. His snout wrinkled away from his teeth. His eyes flashed green in the light.

"Werewolf," Drake said, without opening his door. "Your dog just turned into a freakin' werewolf, Tor."

"He smells the mountain lion," Mr. Barton said, his big lumberjack hands shifting on the wheel. He raised an eyebrow. "Impressive."

Tor scrambled out, forgetting his wrist and yelping as it stung him again. He stepped around the truck and waved at Roscoe with his good hand. Roscoe's big body trembled visibly and he growled again, a rumbling that sounded like a chainsaw getting ready to open up and cut down something big.

"Roscoe, it's okay, it's okay, boy," Tor crooned soothingly. Behind him, Drake opened the door and slid out of the truck. The window rolled down and Gemma's face appeared.

"Wow. That's a big dog," Gemma said. She sounded awed.

"Here's your snowboards. I'll let you talk to your mom, Tor. I need to get this lion out of here so your dog can settle down." Mr. Barton never took his eyes off Roscoe as he grabbed their snowboards and set them on the snowy sidewalk. "He's upset."

"No kidding," Drake said, picking up both snowboards.

"See you tomorrow, kids." Mr. Barton got back into his truck and pulled away so quickly the tires skidded on the icy street before catching. Tor saw Gemma's pale face in the back as the truck drove away, watching him. She looked disappointed in him and he had no idea why.

Tor waited until the truck was a block away before he opened the gate. Of course Roscoe could jump over the silly white picket fence that surrounded their house if he wanted to, but Roscoe was an obedient dog and usually very calm. Cowardly, even, like a gentle giant.

"Hey, Roscoe, you okay?" Tor said gently. Roscoe whined, and as his muzzle relaxed his teeth disappeared. He padded up to Tor and sniffed him, deeply, pressing his nose against him, moving around to Drake, sniffing their arms and hands and legs. Tor thought about what Roscoe must be smelling. Their smells, of course, boy smells. Raine smells too, the girl smell. Mr. Barton, and Gemma, and a hundred winter scents like pine needles and maybe even snow. Over it all, the odor of a wild mountain lion, all over Tor and Drake. And blood. Roscoe sniffed at Tor's hurt wrist and whined.

"Tor?" His mom stood framed in the doorway, her slender figure and her curly brown hair outlined in the warm golden light behind her. "Tor? What are you two doing out there? Come in."

"We had to calm down Roscoe," Tor said, patting his dog on the head with his good hand. Roscoe sighed and leaned against him. "He smelled the mountain lion."

"He about went berserk, Doc," Drake said, giving Roscoe a pat. "He looked like a werewolf. I mean really, a werewolf." He'd taken to calling Tor's mom "Doc," because he couldn't bring himself to call her "Susan" and "Dr. Sinclair" was too formal since he practically lived there.

"There, wolf," Tor said, following Drake to the house.

"Heh. There, castle!" Drake laughed.

"I never should have given you boys that Mel Brooks movie collection," she said with a sigh. "Come on in, adventure boys. I heard someone might need stitches?"

Getting stitched up wasn't as bad at Tor thought it would be. His mom was great. She insisted on studying and good grades and good language and all the mom things, but she seemed to think adventures were what happened to boys. She didn't gasp or cry or anything like that when she peeled back Tor's bloody mitten and saw the gash underneath. She did press her lips together in a thin line of concern.

"You're going to need stitches. And a rabies shot."

"Will I get sick?" Tor fell into a kitchen chair. Drake peeled out of his wet snowboard gear in the utility room and returned to the kitchen in flannel pajama pants and a sweatshirt. He sat on the kitchen floor without a word and started undoing Tor's snowboard bootlaces.

"You won't get sick. It'll make you sore, but not sick."

Roscoe, returned to a normal but extra-large-sized dog, thought Drake sat down on the floor in order to pet him and flopped down at Drake's side. He put his head on Drake's leg and wagged his tail.

"No, dummy." Drake pushed aside Roscoe's head. He pulled at Tor's snowboard boot and it came off.

"Thanks, Drake." Tor wasn't exactly sure how to get out of his snowboard coat without touching his wrist and the thought made more sweat come out on his forehead.

"I'm going to put a big bandage on your wrist. Then Drake and I will take your coat off. It's going to hurt a bit, Tor. I'm sorry."

"Ish okay," Tor said through lips that he'd already pressed tightly together. His mom pressed a pad to his cut wrist and in a moment it was done and he was in his long underwear shirt. The kitchen swirled around him in a crazy way and then everything settled back into place.

His mom unrolled a clean blue plastic pad and took a syringe from another package. Roscoe put his head on Tor's stocking feet and wagged his tail.

"Rabies shots aren't as bad as they used to be, Tor," she said. "You'll get the first one tonight, and a rabies immune globulin shot. You'll be sore, but you won't even miss school."

"Terrific." Tor rolled his eyes at Drake, who smirked.

His mom took his bandaged hand and laid it gently on the table. She removed the bandage and they all leaned in to look. The wound wasn't too long but it was deep, and bloody. The edges were sharp and clean, but they pulled away from each other like opened lips. Inside the cut, Tor could see something white and pebbled.

"Is that his bone?" Drake leaned in closer.

"No, that's just the way skin tissue looks after the capillaries have bled for a while. If this cut had reached bone or ligament, I'd drive Tor to a specialist. Now hold still, this is going to pinch just a bit."

She produced a needle from her other hand like a magic trick and slid it deftly into Tor's skin, right next to the injury. It pinched, all right. Tor bit his lip hard so he wouldn't jump. His mom removed the needle and put it into his skin on the other side of the cut. To make things even worse, she moved the needle around in a circle.

"This is lidocaine, to deaden the nerves." She moved the needle to another spot on his wrist but Tor didn't feel it. The burning, stinging pain was gone.

"Like what the dentist gave me when I had a cavity filled?" Drake asked.

"Same thing. After a minute, when he's totally numb, I'm going to scrub with Betadine. That's going to start the bleeding again, but we need to avoid the risk of infection."

Tor's wrist fell silent at last. It was wonderful not to feel any more. He watched as his mom scrubbed the cut with brownish, yellowish fluid. The wound bled again, but it didn't bother Tor. Drake swallowed hard, but he stayed to watch anyway.

She rinsed his arm and put it on a new fresh pad, changed her gloves to new ones and unrolled a little piece of cloth that held what looked like a row of fishing hooks. "People think skin is thin, delicate. It's actually quite thick and tough." She picked up a hook with a silvery set of pliers. A line of white thread hung down from the hook. She pushed the hook through Tor's skin and twisted the little hook up and through the other side of his cut. "When we do our first operation, as a resident, the surgeon will say 'Make the cut, Doctor.' Then after we make a shallow little cut that doesn't even go through the dermis, the surgeon will say again, 'Okay. Now make the cut.' Then everyone laughs."

"I don't know how you do that." Drake watched her neat, careful stitches with interest, but his face grew pale and he buried his hands in Roscoe's thick fur.

"I think I do." Tor watched his own skin get stitched together and it didn't bother him at all. "I don't know why, but I do."

His mom glanced at him and smiled. She finished the final stitch and tied off the thin thread, snipping it with sharp silver scissors. The cut didn't look all that serious now. It was just a thin line, barely two inches long, with almost invisible stitches along either side.

"Now a nice swab of antibiotic, a tidy little waterproof bandage, and you're right as rain, Tor." She stripped off her gloves. "And the rabies shot. Good thing we keep a supply at the clinic. I'll go pick that up that while you boys eat some food. Drake?"

"I'll make sandwiches, Doc." Drake threw her a mock salute. Roscoe thumped his tail on the floor as Drake stood up. "And food for the werewolf here."

His mom set down two pills and a cup of water on the table.

"Just some pain medicine," she said. "You'll take nothing stronger than ibuprofen after tonight, but it's going to hurt quite a bit tonight." She hugged him fiercely then, and kissed the top of his head. Her arms trembled. "I want to shout at you now that you're safe." Her voice broke a little bit and Tor felt terrible.

"I'm sorry, Mom."

"Oh, I'll be all right. It's a mom thing." She gave him a little shake and let go. "Swallow those pills. Doctor's orders."

Tor felt the drugs moving in and taking hold after he ate his sandwiches and drank two glasses of milk. He hardly noticed the two shots his mom gave him after she returned from the clinic, and as he brushed his teeth, he felt as if something large and soft slowly spun itself around him like a cocoon. Drake looked as tired as he felt, with bloodshot eyes and dark patches under them. Tomorrow was Saturday, at least. They wouldn't have to drag themselves to school. Drake stumbled to Tor's room and crawled into the upper bunk. He gave a huge sigh and was snoring before Tor got under the covers. Tor liked to review his day inside his head before he fell asleep, but too much had happened and the pain medicine made everything fuzzy.

"Roscoe," he said thickly. "Roscoe?" His dog wasn't there.

Tor sat up in bed, fighting against the urge to fall right back into his pillows. Where was Roscoe?

He got out of bed slowly, feeling like he was about twelve feet tall and made of popsicle sticks. Tor could see Roscoe at the end of the hall, staring out the windows. A leaden feeling settled in his belly. In all the excitement about the mountain lion, he'd forgotten something very important. He looked out the window, dreading what he was going to see.

Deep in the woods, a glowing green figure watched him. He'd forgotten about it, but it hadn't forgotten about him.

# Chapter Seven

## Necropsy

Tor stopped at the kitchen entrance. Just for a moment, he remembered what life was like in San Diego before he came to live with his mom. No real friends, a dad who was never there, a stepmom who never ruffled his hair and asked about his homework, twin baby sisters who cried constantly, all while living in a series of boxy houses that looked the same and never felt like home as they moved and moved and moved again because of his dad's real estate business. Here, in Snow Park, he was home.

The old oak floor of the kitchen glowed in the morning sun. His mom sat curled up in her big overstuffed chair in the corner, her clinic papers spread over her lap and her reading glasses perched on her nose. A ribbon of steam rose from her teacup on the little table next to her and Roscoe lay at her feet, his big red-gold body sprawled in a band of sunlight. Roscoe looked up at Tor and his tail thumped lazily against the wooden planks. Drake sat at the kitchen table slurping up a bowl of cereal, his hair tousled and hanging into his eyes. He wore jeans and a cardigan sweater with a bucking horse knitted into the back. Raine sat at the other end of the table, her laptop open and angled away from the bright sunlight coming through the windows. She twirled one of her blue-black braids absently in her fingers as she read. The storm was over and the sky outside the window was a square of pure blue.

"Morning." Drake raised his spoon to Tor and spoke through a mouthful of cereal.

"Good morning. I made a plate for you, honey. Scrambled eggs and sausage. How are you feeling?" Tor's mom put down her pen and peered over her glasses at him.

"I'm lots better." Tor carried his arm gingerly to avoid hitting his bandaged wrist against anything. It didn't hurt nearly as much as it had the night before. "Sausage and eggs? Mom made sausage and eggs? Why are you eating cereal, Drake?"

"Because he already ate his sausage and eggs." Raine snorted. She didn't take her eyes from her laptop.

"I'm hungry. You wouldn't let me eat Tor's portion." Drake rolled his eyes at Raine and flipped back his hair from his eyelashes.

Tor laughed and collected his plate. He didn't know how starved he was until he saw his mom's eggs and sausage and hash browns. The sausage was crisp and popped under his fork as he cut it, and he filled his mouth with a delicious combination of eggs and meat and potatoes and lots of ketchup. His wrist felt tight and sore, but he could handle his fork just fine.

"Here's some ibuprofen, Tor," his mom said, placing two small tan pills by his plate. She set down a glass of juice and ruffled his hair. Then she felt his forehead, seeking fever.

"I'm fine, mom." Tor twitched his head back from her hand. "No fever, see?"

"No fever. Sore muscles, though?"

"Yes. How did you know?" Tor was surprised. He was sore, all over. Every muscle hurt, particularly across his back and shoulders.

"Is that a sign? Of rabies, I mean?" Raine looked up from her laptop, her black eyes narrowed in concern.

"No," his mom smiled. "It's common after any sort of impact trauma. Car crashes are what I'm used to in the emergency room, but this was a lot like one. You were hit by something very big, and every part of your body went into overdrive to survive. Your adrenaline dumped into your bloodstream, your heart rate and blood pressure went through the roof, and you used every muscle in your body to defend yourself. It's as though you ran a marathon and lifted heavy weights, all in a matter of seconds."

"That's what it feels like," Tor mumbled, finishing his breakfast and taking his pills with the juice. He felt sore all over, but he felt okay. His head still had a bump from the library bookshelves the other day and his wrist still hurt, but he was fine.

His mom picked up his wrist and examined the bandage. "Do you feel strong enough to attend the necropsy?"

"Yeah." Tor pulled his wrist out of his mother's hand. Roscoe padded over and pushed his big head under Tor's arm. Tor patted him, working his fingers into Roscoe's silky mane of hair, feeling annoyed. He wasn't sick, and he wasn't a little kid. He didn't need to be babied.

"Then let's bundle up. It's cold out there." His mom began putting her clinic files away.

"You're going?" Tor asked. She grinned like a little girl.

"Are you kidding? A necropsy on a mountain lion? I wouldn't miss it!"

Tor managed to fill and Raine in on the ghostly visit of the night before while they were shoveling the driveway. Or rather, while Drake and Raine shoveled the driveway. His mom was firm. No shoveling for Tor. The snow was heavy and wet, but the time spent shoveling gave them a chance to talk. The roads were already slushy and the sidewalk steamed in the sunshine. Drake threw a shovelful of snow toward Roscoe and he bounded in the air, trying to catch it and woofing happily. A thousand diamonds of light sparkled and flashed in the sunlit layer of snow. Other people were out shoveling too, and on Main Street the bakery was bustling with customers. Old Mr. Martinez came out clutching a bag of pastries and a cup of coffee, wearing a huge brown coat and a red-checked Elmer Fudd hunter's cap.

"Bet that hat's lined with aluminum foil," Drake said to Tor, resting on his shovel.

"Maybe the pastries are for Bigfoot?" Tor asked.

"Stop it, you two. We need to go back to the library." Raine emptied her shovel and smacked it against the driveway to clear it. "Has the ghost come back there? We need to talk to people around town, too. Has anyone else seen it?"

"Yeah, that would be good for our reputations." Drake picked up his shovel and cleared the last of the snow from the driveway. "Excuse me, have you seen a glowing green ghost lately? We're not crazy or anything, ha, ha, why would you think that? They'd all think we were just like Mr. Martinez."

"I think this is all connected." Tor made a snowball and threw it for Roscoe. His dog leaped into the air, surprisingly high for such a big animal, and caught the ball in his jaws. His face was splattered with snow as the snowball exploded in his mouth and he landed, looked comically puzzled. He started sniffing in the drifts to see where the white ball went.

"The mountain lion? How could that be connected to our green guy?" Drake tapped his shovel free of snow and he and Raine smacked their blades together like knights wielding big swords. Tor stuffed his mittened hands into his jacket pocket and felt left out.

"I don't know. I haven't figured that part out yet," he said.

His mom appeared in the garage opening, her slim form wrapped in a big purple parka. A knitted cap covered her hair. She bounced up and down in her snow boots.

"Come on, let's go, we don't want to miss it!"

Raine and Drake exchanged grins with Tor. He patted his leg and Roscoe pranced to his side. Roscoe gave Tor a reproachful look as he pointed at his heated dog bed in the garage, then looked at the car longingly. Roscoe loved car rides.

"Sorry fellow." Tor smoothed his dog's head in his hands and stared into his black-lined, mysterious-looking eyes. "When I come back I'm probably going to smell like that big cat again. Don't go all werewolf on me again, okay?"

Roscoe snorted, sighed, curled around three times, and settled into his bed. Tor gave his dog a final pat, scrambled into the front of his mother's small SUV, and closed the door. Drake and Raine got in the back.

"I love living in this town," Tor's mom commented as she backed out of the driveway. "I don't have to drive unless I'm going for groceries. I don't think I've gotten in this car all week."

"Where's the necropsy being held?" Drake asked.

"Mr. Barton's garage," she replied. "The Bartons live at the edge of town, close to Phantom Canyon road. You know where that is."

They all nodded. Phantom Canyon was one of the canyons that fed the little valley where Snow Park nestled. The other canyons led out of town and across mountain passes but Phantom Canyon was a dead end, a box canyon.

"Wait a minute. In his garage?" Tor asked. He hadn't really thought about where they were going, but he'd imagined some sort of elaborate laboratory, like the ones on television crime shows.

"Well, it's a big garage." His mom smiled. "The doctors in the area don't have anyone who does autopsies in the entire county. We send all our work to Denver, and the lab there isn't very well funded. It's nothing like television, where they have all sorts of fancy gadgets. For veterinary cases? You're lucky to get a slot at all. But the rabies test is common, Tor; we'll know soon. That work is done by a lab and Mr. Barton will get that sample back in a few days."

Tor found himself poking at the bandage on his wrist and stopped. In the distance, skiers and snowboarders floated down the slopes of Snow Mountain, enjoying the brilliant sky and the fresh snow. People filled the chairlifts and traffic clogged Main Street. Cars crunched down the street and shoppers browsed the stores and sipped steaming cups of expensive coffee drinks.

The Barton home sat at the edge of a meadow at the far end of town. Thick woods surrounded the house on three sides and a snow-filled meadow stretched away on the fourth side. A deep, long porch faced the meadow. A big detached garage was tucked behind the home, down the slope, and that was where his mom parked. Mr. Barton came out of the garage door, his big lumberjack face split in a huge grin.

"Dr. Sinclair! Nice to see you again. Tor, Drake, Raine. How's the hand, Tor?" Mr. Barton wore a flannel shirt and jeans, and over that he had on a big black plastic apron, like a butcher's apron. He took off blue latex gloves before he shook their hands.

"Fine, sir," Tor said, but Mr. Barton was already turning away. He smiled at Tor's mom and his clear cheeks reddened. Behind him, Drake rolled his eyes at Tor and tossed his bangs from his eyes. Tor glared back at him. His mom was a very pretty woman, but that didn't mean everyone should get all stupid around her.

They followed Mr. Barton and his mom into the garage, and Tor stopped when he saw the thin body of the mountain lion on a big flat table, stretched out on a blue tarp. Tor could see the cat's face, eyes closed as though sleeping, and the big soft paws that curled up like a sleeping kitten. The sight was at once both awe-inspiring and so sad Tor could barely stand it.

"Nature is neither cruel nor kind." Mr. Barton's hand came down gently on Tor's shoulder. Tor realized they had all stopped and silence had fallen over all of them. "Nature is what it is, and all things happen in their time."

"He's so beautiful," Raine breathed.

"He sure was." Gemma was suddenly at Tor's side, startling him so he jumped. Raine eyed Gemma as the other girl leaned in to look at the big cat. She wore overalls and a flowered shirt. Her red barrettes gave her an unsettling look like she had little horns on each side of her head. Her eyes were squinched into narrow slits of concentration as she stared at the animal. "He was really ill, right, Dad?"

"That's right. I've been doing some preliminary measurements. Let me show you." Mr. Barton pulled blue latex gloves from a box. He handed the box to Tor's mom, who took a pair and handed the box to Tor. Tor looked around at the garage as he pulled on his gloves. The place was as neat as a pin and scrubbed clean. The walls were covered with sheetrock and painted white. A round electric heater sat in the corner, reflecting heat into the room like a big red eyeball. Various shelves and cabinets lined the walls, and two refrigerators sat side by side.

"Feel here, and here," Mr. Barton said. Tor's mom nodded, her face intent, as he guided her hands. Raine reached to feel the same place on the animal's side and so did Drake. Tor put his hand next to theirs. The lion's fur was soft and thick, but under the softness Tor could feel something curved and hard. The lion was perfectly still, and icy cold. This surprised Tor, though it shouldn't, he reminded himself. The animal was dead. He shouldn't expect it to be warm and breathing.

"Are those...?" Drake asked, looking at Mr. Barton.

"His ribs, yes. He was starving. Feel the hip bone, here, and here. Now look at this."

Mr. Barton took the lion's paw in his big hands and gently pushed right in the middle of the main pad. Tor caught his breath as four yellow claws popped out, sharp as razor blades and wickedly curved. "This is the paw that got you, Tor. Still some blood on it, see?"

"Those claws are huge," Raine said, touching one with her finger.

"A mountain lion is built to kill deer," Mr. Barton explained. "They don't run after prey like a cheetah or an African lion. They wait, usually in rocky formations or in trees, and drop on their prey from above. These claws give the lion a good grip so they can use their weight to bring the deer down. Once down, they use their strong jaws to suffocate the animal. It's over very quickly. One deer a week is all this poor fellow needed."

"Why was he starving? There's plenty of deer around here. Turkey too, and rabbits." Raine touched the claw again, and Mr. Barton nodded at the curved length of claw she was touching.

"That's why. Look at this claw. It's just like our fingernails, and it tells the same sort of story."

"Fingernails tell stories?" Drake sounded puzzled.

"Fingernails and hair are a record of our health, Drake," Tor's mom murmured, examining the claw that Mr. Barton indicated. "I see what you mean. Look at this. The nail is ridged. It's also brittle, splintered, crumbling. In a human this would mean anemia, maybe liver disease. He was sick, not just hungry. What about his teeth?"

"Take a look." Mr. Barton peeled up the muzzle of the lion and Tor thought of playing with Roscoe, getting him to look ferocious by lifting his soft muzzle with his fingers and making snarling noises. The lion would never snarl again, and Tor felt another strange burst of sadness that he couldn't explain. If the lion had been healthy, Tor would be lion food right now, and maybe Drake and Raine too.

Something warm touched his arm. He looked down to see Gemma patting him absently. Tor had an image of her helping her dad with the owl that Drake and Raine had rescued years ago, with baby deer and injured foxes and all the animals that could be nursed back to health. She'd probably spent a lot of time helping wounded creatures. She saw him looking at her hand and she withdrew it, her cheeks growing pink.

"The lion's teeth don't look healthy at all," Drake said, leaning in closely.

The lion's big tusks were yellow like the claws, and the gums were red and sore. The lion's tongue wasn't candy pink like Roscoe's. It looked whitish and thin.

Tor's mom reached forward and touched one of the small teeth by the big canine tooth. The tooth wiggled in the sore-looking red gum. It was loose. She took a sharp breath.

"This isn't rabies," she announced. She looked very worried. "This looks like something else."

"Does it look familiar to you?" Mr. Barton let the lion's muzzle go and smoothed it back over the animal's teeth. "Have you seen anything like this?"

"I have, actually," she said, and there was something in her voice that Tor had never heard before. Drake and Raine must have heard it too, because they both looked at her.

"What does it look like?" Mr. Barton asked. "Because I have more than this lion displaying symptoms like this. I have a porcupine, a whole collection of rabbits, a squirrel, and a deer. They were starved, wasted, unable to eat, and with degeneration of the muscles and white coatings on the tongue and loose teeth. When we open this big guy—"

"You'll find tumors," Tor's mom said. Tor realized what he was hearing in his mom's voice. She sounded afraid. Mr. Barton took a breath.

"What is this? You know?"

She put her gloved hands out, and pushed everyone back from the mountain lion.

"It looks like radiation sickness."

# Chapter Eight

## Town Meeting

Tourists packed Kim's Bakery, most of them in ski outfits, drinking hot chocolate or hot coffee and filling their faces with donuts and pastries. Kim's was a popular destination when the slopes started to empty out, and even though the season was almost over, the shop was crowded.

Tor and Drake sat at a table wedged into the back corner next to a carved wooden statue of a bear. A line of dancing bears marched around the painted walls. Stuffed bears with black fur, caramel fur, and brown fur crowded barrels and bins. Bear handbags and bear-shaped candies crowded the shelves above the confection cases that held donuts, croissants, and fudge. If Kim's donuts weren't so delicious, Tor wouldn't be able to take all the touristy bear cuteness.

"This is stupid." Drake crumpled up his napkin into a ball and shot it at the trash container. It bounced off the lip and fell to the floor. He got up to pick it up. "Everyone in town is at that stupid meeting except us."

"We tried to sneak in." Tor shrugged and carefully took another bite of his donut, trying to keep his bandaged wrist from banging against the table. It no longer throbbed with every heartbeat but it still hurt if he knocked it against anything.

"Mr. Stanley ratted us out. That makes it even worse." Drake fell back into his chair. "Caught by the town handyman. It's humiliating."

Tor ate the last bite of his donut and licked his fingers and sighed. He was still hungry, but the line was now out the door. He didn't want to go stand in line again.

"We're the ones who brought the lion in." Drake folded his arms, stretched his legs out, and regarded the two inches of sock between his pants and his shoes. "I'm high-water again. Didn't we just buy jeans?"

Tor leaned over and looked. "Must be the radiation."

"Wow. That was actually funny." Drake looked impressed. "Hey, let's go hang out at Raine's shop. There's no point in getting in line again; the slope litter will buy up all the chocolate donuts anyway."

"She doesn't want us there. My mom told me her parents are at the meeting so she has to handle all the rental returns. And they don't want us helping because of insurance or something." Tor folded his napkin, and folded it again, wishing he had another donut, wishing he could turn himself invisible and go find out what the town grown-ups were talking about, wishing most of all he could stop thinking about his stupid wrist and the word *radiation*.

"Right, they're at the meeting we can't go to." Drake got up. "Come on, let's get out of here."

"Let's go to the library." Tor thought of the old stacks of books that held stories of the *Titanic*, of the moon landing, of Charles Darwin and the Galapagos Islands. Maybe they could find out about radiation. The grown-ups couldn't stop them from doing that.

"Sure, because we haven't spent enough time there lately." Drake sighed dramatically, then clapped a hand to Tor's shoulder. "Actually that's a good idea. We can check and see if Mrs. Harbin wants to watch the footage of the ghost."

Tor shot to his feet. "I forgot about the ghost!"

Everyone in the store turned to look at them. Total silence fell. Tor felt heat flood into his face. The moment stretched out for agonizing seconds until Drake put on a sunny grin. "Yeah, let's go watch that video," Drake said loudly. "It's supposed to be totally scary."

For a moment everyone eyed them, then conversation resumed. Tor worked his way to the exit, his face hot as fire. Drake followed, slipping through the crowd, flipping his bangs away from his eyes and smiling like a celebrity. Outside the store, the air touched Tor's face with a welcome chill. The sun still lit the sky behind the mountains but night was coming quickly. He and Drake headed down the street toward the library.

"Let's see what the library has to say about all this." Drake hauled on the big brass door and ushered Tor in. He pulled out his cell phone and checked it. "Half an hour to closing." The library bustled with customers checking out movies and books. A person was at every computer, their faces lit by the screens, their fingers dancing over keyboards. Tor took a look around and then he and Drake ducked through the doorway that led to the basement stairs.

"First let's check the place where the ghost—" Tor's voice died away and he came to a stop so abruptly that Drake ran into him from behind.

Before them, between the stacks of books they'd put back on the shelves two nights before, lay a body covered by a plain white sheet.

"Hey, watch it. I—" Drake stopped. They regarded what was in front of them. Tor swallowed through a mouth gone paper-dry, his stomach sending nasty quivers through him.

"Photo?" Drake whispered.

"Yeah," Tor said. Drake took out his cell phone and took pictures of the body. Tor cleared his throat. "We should get Mrs. Harbin."

"I'll get her." Drake spun around and sprinted off toward the stairs, leaving Tor alone with the thing in the aisle. He didn't move, didn't hardly breathe, until Mrs. Harbin came hurrying back with Drake at her side, her thin hands twisting together anxiously. She put her hands to her mouth too late to stop a tiny little shriek of dismay from escaping her.

"We have to call the sheriff." Mrs. Harbin made a plucking gesture at the pocket of her gray cardigan, her fingers trembling so badly she missed the opening again and again. "We have to—"

"Wait." Tor peered more closely at the sheet. The head was strangely wrong. He leaned down.

"Don't touch it!" Drake said sharply, but it was too late. Tor took the edge of the sheet and yanked it, hard. The sheet flew up and back, and there in front of them was a body.

The body was made entirely of books. Each book was set in rows and angled to form the outline of a human being, legs out, arms wide, head thrown back.

Mrs. Harbin gave a whistling sigh and her shoulders slumped. "Oh, thank God," she whispered. "I thought—"

"This is still bad, though." Tor dropped the sheet, which drifted to the ground and puddled at his feet. He wiped his fingers on his jeans. "It's super creepy."

"I don't want you to stay in the library tonight." Mrs. Harbin finally found her cardigan pockets with both hands. She shoved them deep and lifted her chin. "Whatever is going on, it's out of your hands. I need to speak to the mayor about this."

"But we—" Tor started.

"I can—" Drake said at the same time. Mrs. Harbin raised her hand in a shushing motion that silenced them both.

"I'm sorry. I never should have involved you. Now you two go on home. I'll come by and speak with your mother later."

Drake turned and walked away down the aisle of books without another word, his shoulders stiff with outrage. Tor nodded at Mrs. Harbin and tried to mumble something polite before he hurried to catch up to Drake. They climbed the stairs and left the library with the last of the day's customers, the air cold enough now to send up plumes from their mouths. Stars shared the night sky with a sliver of a moon.

Tor was surprised steam didn't rise off Drake's head. His friend scowled furiously at the ground and walked so fast Tor had trouble keeping up.

"First the grown-ups throw us out of a meeting that we know more about than they do." Drake kicked at a rock and sent it spinning down the sidewalk. "Then we're thrown out of our own ghost hunting."

"Well, the ghost isn't exactly hanging out at the library any more." Tor peered at the woods at the end of the block past his mom's house, as dark and silent and mysterious as any scary story, and shivered. "I think it knows we're after it."

"Do you think the body—the book thing—the book body was left for us as a warning?" Drake stopped, his hand on the gate to Tor's home. Roscoe appeared around the side of the house where his dog door led into the heated garage. His tail wagged furiously as he trotted towards them.

"Seems like it. Hey, boy." Tor reached around Drake and unlatched the gate so Roscoe could come out. Roscoe pranced out and danced around Tor and Drake, letting himself be petted, his tail lashing their legs.

"Okay, okay, let's go. I need food," Drake announced.

"The lights are on. Mom's home," Tor slipped his fingers underneath Roscoe's collar. "You know what that means."

"Supper?" Drake grinned.

Tor rolled his eyes. "Answers, dummy." Then as they opened the door and the good smells of cooking drifted out, his stomach grumbled loudly. "And food. That too."

Roscoe nudged ahead of them into the kitchen, where Tor's mom tossed noodles and vegetables together in a big wok, a striped apron tied around her waist and her curly brown hair held back by a matching striped band. She gave the noodles a final flip and then turned to smile at them.

"Dinner in just a sec. Get washed up, boys."

"What happened in the meeting?" Tor turned on the sink and gingerly washed his hands, keeping his bandage out of the water. Drake nudged him aside to wash up too.

"Nothing much." Tor's mom took glasses out of the cabinet and set them down on the counter. "Which is what you'd expect from a group of townspeople who have no idea what's going on. Or even if anything is going on." She held up her hand before Tor could interrupt. "There's lots to find out yet."

"But what about the radiation?" Tor demanded.

"We don't know if there is radiation," she said patiently. "We're having tests run on the mountain lion right now. The only possible source of radiation would be the Thayne Mining operation southwest of town. Mr. Thayne was there tonight to answer questions and he seems as puzzled as everyone else."

"I never liked that guy," Drake said, plopping down in his seat and unfolding his napkin. "He always glares at me when he sees me."

"I think he's just a glary kind of guy." Tor's mom smiled at him and ladled bowls of noodles and vegetables. She layered the top with strips of chicken. Tor's mouth watered as she set the bowl in front of him.

"He's the head of Thayne Mining. If we have a pollutant of some kind, his operation would be the first place to look." Tor's mom shook out her napkin and bowed her head. Tor and Drake followed suit, though Tor's stomach grumbled as she spoke a brief blessing.

"So they'll look there first." Tor took a bite and chewed and swallowed, thinking it over. "Right, because ski resorts don't pollute. A mine, yeah, but not a ski slope."

"Well, humans pollute by our very nature." Tor's mom twirled her fork in her noodles, her green eyes distant and thoughtful. "We have to work very hard not to mess up our world. Even a ski resort can pollute the air and water if they don't design their heating and waste disposal systems properly."

"But that's not radiation." Tor swirled up more noodles on his fork and shoveled them in. Drake curled his hands around his empty bowl and sighed.

"That was delicious, Doc."

"Have another bowl, Drake, I made a double batch." Tor's mom smiled and patted Tor on the arm. "You too. Yes, the mining company is more likely to come across a uranium deposit—which they didn't. Or to let their waste processes dump into a local stream—which they haven't."

Tor refilled his bowl and dropped back into his seat. "That means we don't have any leads."

"We have science, Tor. Desmond—Mr. Barton—and I are going to examine the mountain lion again, and we're going to send off samples to different labs, and we'll figure out what's wrong with the animals and that will lead us back to our source, and our enemy."

Drake gave a dramatic shiver. "Our enemy. Sounds like you're tracking down a monster."

Tor's mom smiled at him. "I guess we are. Now off you go to finish homework. Are you going to the library tonight?" Her smile faded as she saw their expressions. "What?"

*** 

"We're not stopping," Tor assured Drake. He blotted at a toothpaste stain on his T-shirt. Stupid wrong hand didn't know how to brush his teeth. When his mom rebandaged it after dinner, the cut looked clean and pink, and the skin around it was normal colored without any swelling. It itched a little, which his mom said was a sign of healing. So he'd be back to using that hand again in a day or so. On the other hand, they still didn't know what killed the mountain lion. Or what the ghost was doing.

"Raine's going to meet us after church tomorrow." Drake sprawled on the bunk, his thumbs racing across his cell phone. "We need to track down Mr. Hayward and tell him what's going on, too."

"If it's something governmental, he'll know. Maybe." Tor shook his head. The old hermit who lived on Phantom Canyon Road worked for the government. He knew a lot of secrets, but he was also as nutty as a Snickers bar.

"We should hunt around the woods to see what we can see, right?" Tor scrambled into his bed and patted the covers. Roscoe climbed up, turned around three times and thumped down, tucking his nose under the soft brush of his tail. Tor reached out and buried his hands in Roscoe's ruff, rubbing up under his ears and smoothing across his face. "You're such a good boy."

"I know," Drake said sleepily from the top bunk. "Everyone tells me so."

"Go to sleep, dork." Tor bunched up his pillow just right and lay down. "See you tomorrow."

"You wake me up if the ghost comes back." Drake said.

"Sure," Tor said, but Drake was already snoring. Tor lay awake for a long time, Roscoe curled up by his side.

# Chapter Nine

## The Disappearing Mountain

The next morning after church, Tor sat on his kitchen floor with Roscoe's big head draped on his lap. Roscoe made a low growling sound of contentment as Tor worked a brush through his dog's fur. The morning sun laid a bright strip of light across the floor and tiny particles of dust danced in the beam. Drake slurped a second bowl of cereal at the table. He wore his brown checkered sweater with the staring kittens printed on it, each of them as big-eyed as an alien.

"Try to relax today," Tor's mom said. She leaned down and kissed Tor above the right eyebrow. She held her clinic notes in one arm. "You know the rules. No straying beyond the town limits. I'll talk to Mrs. Harbin sometime this morning and see what she thinks about you three coming back to your ghost-hunting. You're getting somewhere. I don't think you should quit just because of the creepy book body thing."

"Me neither," Tor said. "Thanks, Mom."

She gave Drake a wink and patted Roscoe, and headed out the door.

Raine showed up a few minutes after Tor's mom left, and immediately went to the fridge. "I know what we need to do," she announced. She opened the refrigerator door in Tor's kitchen and stared at the food inside, her long hair pulled back in a single pony-tail instead of her usual braids. "What we need to do is find out if Thayne Mining is polluting the town." She started pulling bags of cheese and meat out. "Get the bread, we need to make sandwiches for the trip."

"Why?" Tor asked, as Drake got up to fetch the bread from the pan-try. "Why do you think it's them?" He didn't tell her what he really thought, which was that the green ghost that they were hunting was the source of all the weirdness in town. His dreams the night before were filled with rotting green people shambling after him, their glow dis-solving into radiation victims, flesh falling from their bones, moaning and groaning, the living dead trying to catch him and eat him. The two problems had to be connected, the green ghost and the sick mountain lion. Except he'd sound like he was brainless himself if he said any-thing. Ghost zombies?

"Who else could it be?" Drake flipped out slices of bread onto the counter and grabbed the mustard. "There's only one possible polluter, and that's the big strip mine. Thayne Mining."

"What do they mine?" Tor asked, pulling the hair out of Roscoe's brush. Roscoe sniffed the air and got to his feet. He padded over and sat next to Drake with a hopeful expression on his doggy face.

"Molybdenum." Raine started slapping meat and cheese onto the bread slices, her dark eyes squinted into disapproving slits. "It's like another planet on that mountainside, Tor. They strip mine it out, just take the whole mountain out bit by bit."

"What the heck is molyb—molly—what?"

"Molybdenum. Moll-ib-de-num." Drake slipped Roscoe a slice of chicken and the dog took it so quickly and gently Tor didn't have time to slap Drake's hand away. "It's an ore that makes steel harder and stronger. The stuff is valuable and it's sold all over the world."

"So is it radioactive?" Tor put lettuce on the sandwiches and closed them up, sliding them over to Raine for delivery into baggies. They'd done this almost every day during the summer before heading into the surrounding mountains for exploring and fishing and climbing on rocks and generally just messing about.

"Not the ore. But maybe they unearthed something up there, something that's making the animals sick."

"Crazy," Tor muttered, thinking of green ghost zombies.

"Maybe it's like that one book we read, the one with the alien spaceship." Drake picked up two perfectly ordinary apples and looked at them suspiciously. "They dug it up and then all the townspeople started to turn into aliens. Maybe it's like that?"

Tor didn't laugh. "I guess we'll find out." He scooped some dog food into a plastic bag and tied it off. Roscoe got to his feet and his tail started lashing back and forth in joy as Tor dropped the food into his pack. "How do we get there? Isn't the snow too deep to hike?"

"My dad showed me a back trail there a couple of years ago. It's right at the edge of town and it runs across the southern slope of the mountain outside of town," Raine said.

"Southern slope?" Tor asked.

"South-facing. So the snow melts off. That's why all the ski mountain runs are on the north-facing side," Drake said.

"Oh," Tor said. "I never noticed that."

"The mine has a private road and it's closed off so you can't just drive up there. A couple of years ago they had vandals sneak in and spray paint the equipment and break some stuff." Raine slipped her lunch bag into her backpack and filled her water bottle at the sink. "There's a way up a ridgeline in the national forest so no one will see us, and the trail should be clear enough to hike—hey!"

Tor took the bottle that he had just grabbed from her hands and upended it into the sink. Drake stood watching and then he set his bottle gently on the counter with a clink.

"We'll use the bottled water my mom has in the garage. For now." Tor pulled his bottle from his backpack and set it next to Drake's. "Let's not drink town water until we figure this out." Raine pressed her lips together, her eyes worried, and nodded.

"Good thinking. Let's get going. It's a long hike," she said.

\*\*\*

Raine wasn't kidding. Craggy, snow-topped mountains surrounded Snow Park and beyond them were more mountains. The ones to the southeast were particularly forbidding, covered with alpine forests and still choked with snowdrifts. Luckily the sun was out and the air felt almost springlike, warm and moist and full of promise. Tor followed Raine as she picked her way up a mountain trail that led away from town. The trail was mostly dirt except for a few icy patches. Roscoe trotted along with them, happy to be included this time.

Tor took a quick glimpse behind him to see Drake striding along with a smile on his face. He'd pulled a black wool cap over his unruly wheat-blond hair and tucked his boy bangs away. He patted Roscoe with one gloved hand as the dog circled around and nosed at him, tail wagging. Behind Drake, Tor could see Snow Park through the trees, distant and getting smaller, like a tiny miniature town in a Christmas display. They were beyond the town limits, which his mom had just told him not to go beyond, but most of the time her orders were really more like suggestions. As long as he didn't get in trouble, Tor thought, they'd be fine.

"Wait." Raine held up a hand and they stopped. Roscoe padded up next to her and stood sniffing the air. In front of them the faint trail wound around an outcropping of rock and disappeared. The trees were so thick Tor couldn't see into the forest. Raine held her hand up, her gaze intent but unfocused as though she was feeling the forest instead of looking at it.

"You're creeping me out," Drake whispered. "What's up?"

"Nothing. Everything." Raine didn't look back. She started up again and they followed, Tor exchanging a troubled glance with Drake. The day advanced and so did the trail, getting steeper and more faint as they walked up, always up, patchy snow fields on each side but very little on the sun-warmed track they followed. Raine finally stopped for lunch at a flat rock jutting out from the mountain, dry and warm in the sunlight. A mountain pika made cheeping sounds at them but when Tor spotted it, the creature didn't appear to be sick or crazy. The little rodent twitched Mickey Mouse ears at them, then saw Roscoe and made a squeaky sound of dismay. It disappeared under a rock. Roscoe trotted over and nosed around the rock, his tail wagging amiably. Tor finished his sandwich and massaged his calf muscles with his hands, wincing as the stitches in his sore wrist gave a twinge.

"How far?"

"Another hour, but it's because we're going up. It won't take us that long to get home," Raine assured him. She brushed crumbs off her jeans and shouldered her pack. "The snow is mostly off the trail but we might come across some drifts up high. We'd better get going."

They hiked on, Roscoe panting happily at Tor's side, nosing through the rocky terrain as if to see if he could find more squeaky pika. Finally they broke out of the trees and, after hiking across a boulder field of rocks and patchy snow, Raine stopped and dropped to one knee, gesturing for them to follow her.

They crawled to a rocky outcropping. Tor could tell they were at a high elevation. His heart beat stronger than usual and his breath came faster. There wasn't as much air up here. The sun blazed white above them and the skies around were blue, empty of a single cloud. Snowfields covered the hillside. Underneath Tor's gloves the rock felt icy cold. Raine slowly raised her head and glanced back, making a gesture to Tor. He frowned and then, understanding, got out his black stocking cap and pulled it over his hair.

"Is somebody going to shoot at us?" Tor whispered to Drake.

"After the vandals broke all that equipment they got real serious about security, so nobody even makes field trips here any more." Drake made a come-on gesture with his hand. "They'd arrest us for sure if they caught us on their property."

"We're not on their property," Raine said. "There's a perimeter road down the slope from us on the other side. That's the boundary line of their property. But we should still be careful."

Tor crawled up next to Drake and Roscoe followed, wriggling on his stomach like a furry commando.

Tor's amusement at his dog fell away as the valley below came into view. His hands gripped the icy cold rocks as the sun beat down on his black hat, making his head uncomfortably warm.

"Horrible, isn't it?" Raine rested her chin on her hands. "They're eating a mountain."

Below him a stark, bare pit yawned, covering the entire valley floor below, miles and miles across. The mountain on the other side of the valley was half gone. Trucks rumbled up and down spiraling roads that lined the pit, filled with gray-looking rubble. Tor spotted a truck stopped at a big gate. The trucks were as big as buildings. The wheels must be as big as his mom's car. And there were hundreds of them, driving up and down the bare earth, carrying away the ore to a set of gray buildings that nestled at the edge of the pit.

"Thayne Mining." Drake waved his hand. "They've been digging away at this mountain since before we were born. Won't stop until it's gone, I guess."

"I didn't know this was here." Tor put a hand into Roscoe's fur and sank his fingers into his dog's sun-warmed ruff. "This is crazy."

"There's no highway through the mountains to here, just the mine. So no one sees it unless they let you. And they don't let anyone in here anymore."

"What's that?" Tor pointed at a suspiciously green swath of meadow to the south of the mine, away from the dusty pit and the chewing trucks.

"Mine reclamation," Raine explained. She put her hand up and traced a curve of mountain through bare space. "The mountain looked like this, once."

"Do that again." Tor watched as she traced a big curve across the bare space in front of him, sketching the way the mountain looked a generation ago, before Thayne Mining decided to eat it all up. "Wow. That's terrible."

"They own it. It's their property, just like Borsh Mountain is my family's property." Raine crossed her arms and rested her chin on them, her black eyes scanning the pit in front of them. "They're going to eat it all up, and eventually nothing will be left but a grassy meadow. It's sad."

"Here's the problem." Drake huffed out a sigh. "I don't see anything that looks any different than the field trip I took in the fifth grade. No spaceship sticking out of the ground."

"No glowing lake of poison." Raine narrowed her eyes and scanned back and forth over the pit. "Nothing but trucks and ore and dust."

"Can we get any closer?" Tor knew the answer before Raine shook her head. The slopes below them were north facing and covered with a thick blanket of snow with a few rocks poking out here and there. A dirt road snaked across the slope, marking the boundary of the mine property. A pika scrambled on a rock below them and sat with little round ears twitching, nibbling at a piece of grass. Roscoe raised his head, watching the creature. Anything bigger than the pika would stand out. They'd be spotted before they got halfway to the big fence that surrounded the site.

"Maybe we could come back at night," Drake suggested. "Or—"

"What's that?" Tor interrupted.

A man came out of the gray buildings, his black suit like a tiny slash of ink against the dusty background. He made a gesture like he was throwing a baseball.

"What's he doing?" Raine asked.

The object he threw rose in the air and then didn't arc down like it should. It continued up, wobbling a little, catching the sun and throwing off a sparkle of light. The man pulled something from his pocket and held it in his hands like a controller to a video game, but Tor couldn't tell what it was at that distance.

Then he knew, and his stomach clenched in cold fear.

"What is that?" Drake asked.

Tor reached out and grabbed his friend's arms, hauling them back from the rocky edge.

"They spotted us. That's a drone. They sent a drone after us."

# Chapter Ten

## Hiding from the Sky

They raced across the snowy boulder field, the sheltering trees an impossible distance ahead, the heat of the sun beating down at them from the clear blue sky. Tor could hear nothing but his racing heartbeat and his labored breath, harsh and hot in the thin air.

"Hurry!" Drake called back, his longer legs covering the ground in big strides. Raine ran behind Drake, her ponytail bobbing, and Roscoe followed her. Tor tried to keep breathing and keep running, even though every breath stabbed into him now. He couldn't keep up the pace much longer.

Drake took a sharp turn downhill and disappeared. Raine followed. Tor spotted the rock overhang his friends had just ducked under and skidded in beside them as a thin, wasplike sound rose to a shriek in the skies. The drone was coming.

"Where is it? Does it see us?" Tor hunched up next to Roscoe. The dog panted, slobbering on Drake's shoes. The rock was just a big boulder perched on another one, creating a pocket of cold shadow underneath.

Roscoe's tail was in the sunlight. Tor tucked it next to Roscoe's body, out of sight.

"I don't know if it spotted us." Raine had already caught her breath and wasn't even sweating. As she looked out into the sunlit boulder field, Tor knew the signs of his friend. Raine was furious. Tor looked at her instead of outside, because he couldn't see up unless he leaned out and exposed his face to the drone, and the desire to look out was maddening. How far away was it? The bitter smell of wet earth and cold stone filled the shadows.

"Is it armed, do you think?" Tor asked. Drake made a chuffing sound.

"Really? Armed? What do you think this place is?" Drake asked.

"A military grade ore facility. I don't know, maybe Homeland Security gave them drones to protect themselves." Tor felt his face grow hot with embarrassment. "I don't know."

"Tor's right." Raine tilted her head back and forth, producing an audible pop from her neck. "The drone might be armed. It definitely has a camera on it. We can't let it see us. They'll arrest us, or worse. If they're the ones responsible for the poison that made that mountain lion sick, they might do anything to cover it up."

Drake clenched his jaw. "They could make us disappear and no one would ever know."

"We can't stay here," Tor pointed out. "They might send guards to look for us."

"So we can't go, and we can't stay. What do we do?" Drake tried to straighten his head but it hit the overhang. He winced. "I'm turning into a pretzel here."

"We run," Tor said. "As soon as we hear the drone move away. Leapfrog to the next overhang, then to the next, until we get to the trees."

"Right." Raine reached for her plastic water bottle and took a long drink. "Can you see down the trail, Drake?"

Drake hunched himself around to the very edge of the shadow and squinted. "There's another overhang, not too far away."

Tor could hear the thin whine of the drone echoing off the rocks as it tracked back and forth across the sky. He couldn't see it, but he imagined a long stinger dripping with poison, bug eyes searching for them, ready to stab and sting.

"We run for the trees." Drake bunched his legs under him. "I'm going to duck out and see where it is. Get ready to run."

"Ready." Raine holstered her water bottle.

"Ready." Tor sunk his fingers into Roscoe's mane, ready to urge his dog to run.

Drake stood up slowly, his eyes just above the rock overhang. "We can make it. Let's go!"

Raine, Tor, and Roscoe scrambled out and followed Drake, who bounded down the rocky slope. Tor's heart pounded in the high altitude and he tried to listen for the shriek of the drone. They slid under the next rock overhang while the drone searched down the slope from them. Tor could see it now, a tiny boxy shape with four propellers on the top. It glinted gold in the sunlight.

Roscoe, sitting next to him and panting happily, suddenly raised his ears and became still, his eyes fixed on something close to them. Tor stopped breathing. Had the mine sent out security guards to find them? He turned his head in the same direction Roscoe was staring.

A tiny pika observed them from underneath a rock close to them, its little round ears twitching, eyes as bright and black as drops of oil.

"Hey, pika." Drake grinned at the little animal.

"Next overhang." Raine pointed. "It's pretty far away. But I don't see anything closer."

Tor kept his hand in Roscoe's warm fur so his dog wouldn't try to make a meal out of the little pika. The pika didn't seem afraid, which worried Tor. He remembered the mountain lion and how it wasn't afraid of them, either. Was the pika sick like the mountain lion? At least it couldn't eat them.

"We can do it." Drake smacked Tor on the arm.

"Let's go." Raine got up first this time and leaped from rock to rock, her ponytail shining in the sunlight and her backpack bouncing up and down. Tor urged Roscoe on and they followed.

They were almost to the rock overhang when the drone's motors started coming closer. Tor couldn't tell if the drone spotted them or if it was just moving upslope to search. He ran faster and they tumbled into a pile under the rock all out of breath, even Roscoe. No one spoke as they panted and listened for the drone. It got closer and Tor hunched under the rock so far his head banged against the rock right where he'd gotten the lump from the library shelves. The stitches in his wrist throbbed as though they might break open, and his sweaty back itched under the backpack right where he couldn't reach it. His calves hurt from all the hiking and running and his feet throbbed.

"I want to kill that drone," Tor muttered.

"Me, too." Drake didn't look any happier than Tor felt. His knuckles dripped blood where he'd scraped them on a rock somewhere. Raine looked calm and cool, but Tor could see the muscle of her jaw clenched tight.

"Here it comes," Tor whispered. He forgot his aches and pains as the drone engine buzzed closer and closer.

"Hold." Drake put his hand on Roscoe's ruff, next to Tor's. "Don't move."

The whine filled the air and Tor clenched his teeth, waiting for the machine to drop down in front of them and stare at them, bulging eyes taking pictures of them. They'd get arrested for sure. He'd be grounded for life.

Raine opened a flap of her pack and slowly withdrew her slingshot, a whittled length of aspen with a pouch of deerskin for a cup that her father had made for her. She carried it with her all the time, though she never took it out or used it on anything in front of them. She told Tor once it was a real hunting weapon and it wasn't for play. Now she picked up a small rock and fitted it into the pouch, pulling the springy woven lashes tight. Tor nodded and so did Drake. What a great idea. If the drone found them, their best bet was to destroy it.

Drake eased back against the rock, pressing tight, giving Raine room to move.

The moment stretched out and the drone motor filled his head and made Tor's teeth ache, and he couldn't tell it was moving away until Drake sighed and softened, his head hanging forward, his hair in his eyes.

"It's going. It didn't find us." Raine released the tension on her slingshot. Her hands trembled a bit as she stuffed the ancient weapon back into her pack. "I was hoping I wouldn't have to shoot. I haven't really practiced too much with this."

"Maybe you should." Tor gave a shaky laugh. "Okay. Let's get to those trees."

The drone buzzed away down the hill as they ran for the sheltering trees. They were in the shadows before they had time to run out of breath.

"Excellent!" Drake high fived Tor, then Raine. "Now all we have to do is—"

He stopped because Raine held up her hand. She tilted her head to one side, listening hard, and her mouth thinned into a grim line.

"Engines. I hear engines," she said.

"They sent a patrol after us." Tor smacked his fist into his palm. "They sent someone after us."

"We can't outrun a truck," Drake said. "Or an ATV if they sent one of those. We're going to get caught."

# Chapter Eleven

## Wild Brother

"We're not getting caught." Tor shook out Roscoe's leash and clipped it to his collar. "Raine, is there a road close to us?"

"Not that I know of." Raine searched the trees with her hand to her brow to block the dappled sun. The afternoon light speared through the trees and made irregular patches of gold and green in the sun-warmed pines. Snowdrifts filled the hollows and shaded spots. Snow in the sunlight trickled water as it melted. The small sounds of water running from a thousand different places made the laboring engine of the approaching truck sound close, then far away.

"I can't tell where they're coming from," Drake whispered. "Can you?"

"Not yet. We need to get further down this trail." Raine struck off at a rapid pace, her feet quiet and swift on the rocky trail. Tor followed with Roscoe panting at his side, the faint sound of engines swelling, then fading. "We're upwind, that's why we can—"

She stopped so abruptly Tor ran into her, and Roscoe ran into him, and Drake nearly fell over Roscoe, which was so funny that Tor almost started laughing. Then he saw Raine's expression.

"What is it?" he asked.

She pointed, and Drake drew a quick, gasping breath. Tor spotted a big black dog on the trail ahead of them, standing at the bottom of the slope where the trees thinned out into a clearing. The dog walked into the sunlit meadow and put its head down and sniffed at some grasses.

Roscoe's mane bunched up against Tor's hand and his dog made a tiny whining sound. "It's just a dog, you big baby," Tor whispered.

"Not. A. Dog," Drake whispered through clenched teeth, standing stiff and still as though afraid the dog would see them. Raine, too, stood absolutely still as though she was afraid the creature was a bear or some—

Tor's stomach fell right down into his hiking boots. The dog down the trail from them wasn't a dog at all. It was a bear.

"Back up slowly," Raine whispered, so softly Tor could hardly hear her. "No sudden movements."

Behind Tor, Drake stepped backward one step at a time, his breath harsh and fast.

"That's a big bear," Drake whispered.

"It doesn't look like a bear," Tor whispered back. "It's skinny. Aren't bears supposed to be fat?"

"It looks sick," Raine whispered, a bare thread of sound. "Like the lion." Down in the sunny meadow, the bear slowly padded over to a fallen log. Suddenly it dug furiously with big black paws into the rotted wood. Chips flew back and then the bear stuck its nose into the log, snuffling. It raised its head and looked around as though confused. Tor's fingers felt numb and cold with fear. If it spotted them…

"We're upwind," Drake breathed. He kept stepping back and Tor followed, Roscoe keeping pace with them, his head up and his nose sniffing at the air. Tor was glad Roscoe didn't bark. His dog's usual silence was saving them.

"Keep going." Raine made gestures with her hands to keep shooing them back. Tor turned around and the last bit of trees thinned out in

front of him, back to the rocky slope and the pikas and the waspy drone
and the unseen men coming closer and closer to them.

"We can't keep going, Raine," Tor whispered. "We have to stop or
we'll break out of the trees again."

"Let's head downslope that way." Drake pointed into the trees, off
the trail, away from the snuffling bear. "We can find the trail later."

"Famous last words," Raine muttered, shifting from one foot to the
other. She gripped her backpack straps so tightly her knuckles looked
like sharp white stones against the smooth skin of her hands. "We
shouldn't leave the trail. Let's wait until the bear moves on. We can—"

An engine roared off to their right and that answered that. Raine
broke into a trot down the slope and to the left, leaving the trail and
keeping her feet on the bare rocks. Tor and Roscoe followed with Drake
right behind, trying to keep as swift and silent as their Ute friend, avoid-
ing the snow that would leave a clear trail. Roscoe galloped along with
them, tongue hanging out, his big paws as silent as the bear. Behind
them Tor could hear the truck, the squeak and rattle of suspension and
the crunch of tires on fallen branches and drifts of snow. He didn't dare
to look back, afraid to see men jumping out and racing after them or,
worse, aiming rifles at them.

Raine came to a skidding stop and this time Tor and Roscoe didn't
pile into her back. She panted silently, her eyes wide and white in her
face, and she pointed.

They hadn't escaped the bear after all. While they were racing down
the slope to escape the truck noise, the bear had done the same thing,
trying to get away from the sound of humans. The creature stood less
than a dozen yards away. Tor could smell the musky, bitter scent of it. It
lifted its black nose, head pointed up the slope and away from them. They
were upwind of it still, barely, and the slender boles of pine trees made
a thin screen between them. It wasn't enough, not nearly. Roscoe leaned
into Tor's side, shivering, his breath hot against Tor's hand as he panted.
Drake stood perfectly still next to him, and Raine was an unmoving girl
shape, her eyes glinting as she scanned back and forth through the trees.

Up the slope and beyond the trees came the sound of truck doors squeaking open. A truck door slammed. Tor heard men's voices, tense and brusque, one of them barking orders. The three of them were too far away to hear clearly what the men were saying, but their voices were close enough to send electric wires of hot and icy cold stabbing through Tor's insides.

The bear lifted its dark nose and sniffed the air. Clumsy-looking paws with enormous white claws shifted back and forth on the ground nervously. The bear's mouth opened and it licked the air with a surprisingly pink tongue.

Just like that, Tor had an idea. Stupidest idea ever, probably, but they might have a chance to get away if it worked. He reached into his front pocket, slowly, and pulled out a baggie with his lunchtime energy bar, made of dried fruit and nuts molded into a rectangle. He gestured at Raine, pulling his hand back to his cheek and letting it go. Raine stared and him and shook her head. Tor broke a piece of the bar off and held the chunk out to her, then made the same gesture again.

"Hungry," he mouthed, and rubbed his stomach. "Hungry!"

Raine's eyes lit up and she pulled out her slingshot. Tor handed the chunk of fruit-and-nut bar to her, his fingers trembling so badly he nearly dropped it. She snatched it and put it in her slingshot cup, pulling it back to her cheek. There was no time to waste. Tor could hear crackling sounds as the searchers started into the trees. They were minutes, maybe seconds away from being caught. Drake put a hand on his arm and gripped hard as Raine let the slingshot go. The chunk of food sailed through the air silently and landed in the pine needles just ahead of the black snout of the bear.

Tor handed Raine another chunk of the bar. The bear was still sniffing the air suspiciously. It hadn't detected the morsel of food.

Raine's next shot put a piece of nut-and-fruit bar a foot ahead of the bear. This time the bear's nose wrinkled up immediately and it started snuffing around the pine needles. In a moment it found the food and crunched it up, then snuffled until it found the first piece. The bear pawed at its head and shook it as though confused. Then its nose wrinkled again and it crunched up the morsel of food.

Tor handed Raine another chunk and this time her shot brought the bear up the slope, toward the searchers. The animal was now on the trail of delicious dried fruit and mixed with almonds, cashews, and honey. And what bear didn't like honey?

Two more chunks of food landed just ahead of the black bear and as Drake pulled Tor and Roscoe away from Raine and down the slope step by careful step, Raine launched a final piece of the bar and turned to follow them. She skidded a bit on the slippery needles.

"Go, go," she mouthed. "Quick!"

Tor took the lead. They plunged down deeper into the trees and away from the bear. Tor took a glance back and couldn't see the bear or hear anything.

Drake grabbed at his arm and Tor came to a stop, Roscoe panting beside him, and Raine gestured at them to huddle behind the trunk of a giant old pine tree.

"Wait," Raine whispered.

In the distance, not very far away, Tor heard a surprised shout and then a sound he'd never heard outside the movies before. Something roared, deep and so huge the entire forest seemed to shake.

"The bear," Drake mouthed. "Whoa."

Roscoe shivered and shook his shoulders as his fur stood up in a stiff ruff around his head. His snout wrinkled back in a snarl and a rumble started up in his chest like a big engine idling.

"No, Roscoe." Tor laid a gentling hand on his dog's head. "Hold, boy."

The bear roared again as another shout echoed through the trees. Doors slammed and a horn blared twice, three times. Engines whined and receded down the slope, faster than they'd come, and a crash and tinkle sounded like the vehicle glanced off a tree in a panic and lost a bumper or a rearview mirror. Then there was silence. They were gone.

"That was awesome." Drake clapped a hand on Tor's shoulder.

"They'll think it was the bear, maybe, instead of us out there." Tor urged Roscoe to follow as Raine slipped from behind the tree and made her way down the slope.

Raine pointed to the faint outline of the trail down through the trees. "There it is. Let's get home quick. We have to talk to your mom, Tor. I have an idea."

# Chapter Twelve

## The Consulting Detective's Smarter Brother

"**M**ore scrapes? You teenagers go through so many bandages." Tor's mom held out her hand and waited until Drake reluctantly put his hand into hers. His knuckles were scabbed over. The blood had caked in his skin and darkened under his fingernails. She examined his hand closely. "Go wash that in the kitchen sink so I can medicate it. Tor?"

"I'm fine, Mom," Tor protested, but his mom pointed to a kitchen chair. She was dressed in yoga pants and a T-shirt, and her curly hair was tied up in a bun on the top of her head. Her cheeks were still flushed from her workout but her eyes were stern. Drake walked over to the sink to wash up and Roscoe trotted to his water bowl and began lapping. Raine sank into a chair, letting her backpack slide to the floor next to her. Tor sat down where his mom directed, his legs feeling rubbery after the long hike home. His head throbbed where he'd bumped his old library bruise against the rock when they were hiding from the drone.

Chicken noodle soup bubbled in a crockpot next to the stove. Tor's mouth started watering at the delicious smell as his mom unwrapped his wrist and looked closely at his stitches and his healing wound.

"Looks good. Raine, any injuries?"

"Just my head."

Tor's mom snapped upright in her chair.

Raine threw up her hands. "Just kidding, I'm not hurt. I mean my brain hurts from all the questions that we don't have answered."

"Oh." Tor's mom sighed and rewrapped Tor's wrist snugly. "I know. I've been studying my medical journals and half the time I've found myself staring out the window trying to figure out what's happening around here. I couldn't even focus in yoga class today. Drake, your knuckles."

Drake exchanged a glance with Tor as he sat down after washing his hands. Raine nodded in agreement and so did Tor.

"We want to talk to you," Raine said, after taking a deep breath. "We decided we needed someone who—"

"Believed." Drake said.

"Believed in what?" Tor's mom bent over Drake's hand and moved his fingers back and forth. "It's a deep scrape, but it doesn't need stitches. I'll put some ointment on it."

"You believed in the curse that was on the town. We broke it together," Tor said. He glanced at Raine and she gave him a tiny nod that meant *go on*. "So you might believe in the ghost too."

She grinned at them. "Oh, yes, the ghost!" Her smile fell away as she observed their expressions. "Wait, there's really a ghost?"

"Yes, there is. I think everything that's been happening is all connected somehow." Tor gestured at Raine to continue. He got up to put food in Roscoe's bowl.

Raine leaned forward. "We've been running around in circles ever since Tor got jumped on by that sick mountain lion. We need to talk over what's been going on, and we need someone who won't—" She paused.

"Scoff." Drake examined his knuckles, now glistening with ointment, and flashed his famous grin at Tor's mom. "And can we get some food while we're talking?"

She regarded them, and then held up her hand. "Okay. Let's get dinner and I will hear you out. I'll be—Sherlock Holmes' smarter brother. I'll be your Mycroft Holmes."

Raine laughed. "Exactly!"

Tor exchanged glances with Drake and they shrugged in unison. "Sounds good to us," Tor said.

Tor's mom got up from the table. "Raine, let your folks know you're here for dinner. Then both of you wash your hands and we'll set the table."

Roscoe, having finished his food, turned around three times and collapsed into his bed. Tor's mom served up the chicken soup as Raine dug out her cell phone. The air filled with the aroma of fresh baked bread as Tor's mom opened the oven and lifted out a tray. Tor's stomach growled and Drake sighed happily.

"Okay," Tor's mom said, after they sat down together. "Bow your heads." They all bowed. "The short version today. God bless this meal. Okay. Let's start."

"You know we were in the library two nights ago," Tor started. He spooned up some soup and nodded at Drake to continue.

"We saw a real ghost," Drake said through a mouthful of crusty bread. Tor reached out and took some slices to dunk into his soup.

Tor's mom kept her face expressionless. Drake took another bite and tilted his head towards Raine. She finished swallowing her food before she spoke.

"So we saw it in the library but it escaped and nearly killed us all—" Raine stopped and waved her hands. "Not really, some books fell on Tor and me—"

Tor remembered the heavy metal shelves crashing down on them, and the smothering darkness of hundreds of books burying them. A few books. Right.

"So by the time we got home it was late, and the next day was school, so we decided to visit our secret valley after school and talk things over. Then mountain lion, grrr, roar, slice," Drake said. He reached out his bowl and Tor's mom ladled out more soup. The soup sent up ribbons of warm steam in the kitchen. Behind Tor, Roscoe gave a buzzing snore.

"Then the lion died." Raine tapped her fingers on the table, her dark eyes narrowing in thought. "The necropsy was Saturday, and now it's Sunday. Everything's happened so fast."

"That first night, Friday, and then the next, I saw the ghost in the woods, watching the house," Tor confessed.

"Our house?" his mom asked, raising her eyebrows. Her green eyes darkened with worry and her fingers twined together nervously, but then she smoothed her hands down on the table again. Tor knew she was trying to be Mycroft Holmes. She wouldn't scoff at them or yell at them, not until she'd heard the whole story.

Including the part about how he'd left the town limits to hike to the Thayne mining pit. Tor swallowed hard and gave a tiny nod to Raine.

"We hiked to the Thayne mine today—that's why we were gone all day." Raine gave a sidelong look at Tor. "I know it's out of town limits but it's not, well, far." She described their journey and their escape from the drone and the sick bear.

Tor's mom stared down at her fingers, her lips pursed. Finally she raised her head. "Did you see anything at the mine?"

"No." Drake shook his head, his wheat-colored hair hanging over his eyebrows. "No lakes of poison, no alien spaceship, nothing."

"So now where are we?" Tor's mom asked, one eyebrow raised. Tor felt the tightness leave his shoulders. She might ground him later for going on the hike to the mine, but she wasn't going to yell at him now.

"We think the appearance of the green ghost has something to do with the way the mountain lion looked. And the bear, on the trail. He looked sick, thin. I read about radiation poisoning. I know it doesn't actually make you glow green—" Tor said.

"No, it doesn't." Tor's mom smiled a little. "And it wasn't radiation. Our local friend Mr. Hayward happens to have a Geiger counter and he brought it in to check out the mountain lion."

Tor felt a great yawning relief swallow him up to the neck. It wasn't radiation. He trusted Mr. Hayward. The old guy looked like a backwoods hermit but he used to work for the government. He was nutty, but he was a good guy.

"Oh, good," Raine said, expelling a gusty sigh. Drake heaved a sigh too, and behind them the sleeping Roscoe made a grumbling snore that might have been agreement. They all laughed a little. The kitchen seemed warmer now, brighter, and Tor's wrist stopped itching for the first time.

"If it wasn't radiation, what was it?" Drake asked.

"After we removed radiation as a suspect I began to think of mercury poisoning. Mercury is a naturally occurring metal but it can collect in runoff from mining or industrial plants. The symptoms include lack of coordination, dizziness, and confusion."

"Runoff from mining? Like the Thayne mine," Raine said in a low voice.

"But they don't have collection pools from the mining process," Tor's mom said, her brow furrowed. "Mr. Thayne was at the town meeting and said so. They ship it off to a hazardous waste recycling place to get rid of it. And your hike today just confirmed what he insisted. No collection pools for mercury to gather. So it's not mercury poisoning."

"So we don't know what the sickness is. But the ghost appeared at the library right around the same time that Gemma said her dad started seeing sick animals," Raine said.

"That's right." Tor snapped his fingers. "Mrs. Harbin came to talk to us after a couple of weeks of the ghost pulling the books out and leaving the puddle of water. And Gemma was acting all weird at school all that time."

"Well, weird-er," Drake said with a snort.

"This sounds like a connection," Tor's mom said. "The animals might be getting sick from contaminated water. If the ghost is leaving puddles behind, that could be something. If only I could see it."

"Raine has pictures of it," Tor said. "Maybe that would help?"

Tor's mom threw up her hands. "What? Definitely!"

Raine dug her cell phone from her backpack and handed it to Tor's mom. She examined it and gave a satisfied nod. "This is compatible with the television. Let's see it on the big screen." They followed her into the living room and Drake lowered himself into a couch, groaning as he sank back into the pillows.

"You're about to burst, you ate so much," Raine grumbled as Tor's mom fiddled with a cord and the side of the flat screen television.

"I was hungry." Drake folded his arms behind his head. "I almost starved to death today."

Tor snorted and started to say something when the screen popped into life and there, nearly as big as they were, stood the library ghost.

They all flinched, even Tor's mom. The picture was a blurry but even so, the ghost was realer than real, completely without hands or feet or a face, hovering in the bookshelf aisle and giving off a sickly green glow.

"There's more pictures," Raine said. Tor's mom found the forward button. The ghost leaped back, jumped through the bookshelves and disappeared in a series of photos and then Raine's phone tumbled to the ground. There were no more pictures.

"That's a real ghost, right?" Drake asked. "Right?"

"Let me look at these again." Tor's mom stood close to the screen and clicked through the pictures again. Then again. Roscoe wandered in and flopped onto the carpet next to Tor. Outside, the dark pressed against the windows and a wind rattled a pane of glass somewhere in the house.

"What do you think, Doc?" Drake asked.

"I think this is a very professional job, like something from a movie." Tor's mom took the phone from Raine and paused it at the picture where the ghost started to leap backward.

"What?" Tor said, leaning forward. "Really?"

"You mean you don't think it's real?" Raine protested.

"Wait, let me finish," Tor's mom said, holding up a hand. "It could also be a real ghost."

They all settled back into their couch cushions, but Tor still frowned and so did Drake and Raine.

"You didn't see it," Drake said in a low voice. "Or feel the cold."

"I didn't. But I know there are some very expert people who could have created this ghost, given time and equipment. I'm a doctor. We don't guess at what's wrong with people, we test them, and then we test them again."

"But why?" Tor burst out. "Why would someone pretend to be a ghost?"

"And if it's real, why is it haunting the library?" Raine asked. "Either way, real or fake, we have someone doing something to the library."

"And staking out our house now," Tor said. His mom paled a bit and settled into her armchair. Roscoe usually padded over to get a pat or two when she did that but he was completely out, exhausted, snoring on the floor next to Tor.

Tor's mom tapped her finger against her lips, her brow creased. "I agree they might be connected. Like my dumb little brother Sherlock says, when you have eliminated the impossible, whatever remains, however improbable, must be the truth."

Roscoe twitched his paws in his sleep and made a low growling sound. Tor's mom smiled down at him and then checked her watch. Her eyebrows went up. "It's getting late. We still have more questions than answers, but we at least have a start. And it's a school night. Off to home with you, Raine."

"We'll walk her home," Tor said. Raine gave him the beginnings of an offended look but then she shrugged wearily instead.

"Okay. Whatever."

Roscoe clambered to his feet and stood with his tail wagging slowly, clearly not ready for another adventure but willing to go, like a tired soldier called back to duty.

"Do you have a—Mycroft idea?" Raine asked Tor's mom. She smiled at them.

"I do, I think."

"Well?" Drake said.

"You've spent all this time chasing the ghost, trying to catch it. But maybe it might be trying to warn you about the sickness. So instead of trying to trap it…" Tor's mom put her hands on her hips and gave them a small smile. "The next time you see it, why don't you *talk* to it?"

# Chapter Thirteen

## Principal Crandall Turns on the Megaphone

"Well, this isn't good." Tor stared down at the water fountain in the school hallway. Yellow tape wrapped around the old white porcelain fountain. A sign hung above: "Out of Order." Noise in the hallway was even more deafening than usual as Drake and Tor stood looking at the fountain. Drake gave Tor a shrug with one shoulder, where his backpack held two purified drinking water bottles from Tor's home. Tor had the same tucked into his pack. They weren't drinking the town water until this was all figured out. Still, it gave him a chill to see the tape over the homely water fountains in the old school.

Someone elbowed by and broke his focus on the fountain. The class bell was about to ring. He gave a nod to Drake and hurried off, searching for Raine's shiny black hair in the crowds and failing to spot her. Well, he'd see her at lunch or during choir that afternoon. Everyone was required to sing in the choir. Tor secretly enjoyed it, though he complained that he hated it along with everyone else.

He dropped into his seat in his first class just as the bell rang. Mrs. Petrus stalked back and forth like a bird, tall and knobby and fierce. Finals were coming up and she acted as though if they didn't all write perfect essays about Shakespeare and George Eliot they would all be sent to prison or something. She peered over her beaky nose at the class and they shushed immediately.

"Before we get to work, as your first period teacher I have a notice to share with you." She gave an irritated little cough. "The water fountains have been turned off until the town determines if there's some sort of pollutant causing a problem with the water supply. They don't know, but they're being cautious, so they're asking us to boil water at home. If you brought water with you today we'll ask you to pour it out."

Snow boots shuffled and a few clicks of pens made little nervous sounds in the room, but no one spoke. Tor realized that everyone must know about the mountain lion attack on him and the disease it seemed to have. They didn't know about the ghost, but maybe some of the other kids in school had seen strange things too, or experienced something. It gave him a funny feeling, as if people were watching him without him knowing about it. He spotted students giving him side-long glances and he held himself still so he wouldn't slouch down in his chair. Underneath the bandage on his wrist, his healing cut started itching again.

"We have a generous donation of distilled, bottled water from Thayne Mining available in the cafeteria. We should know what's going on in a few days."

Tor's blood pounded but he didn't move, didn't shuffle, didn't even twitch. Thayne Mining, the people who'd chased them with a drone and then with men with guns…

We never saw any guns, Raine's voice spoke in his head, and he wanted to argue with her but she wasn't really speaking inside his head and anyway, she was right. They hadn't even seen the security forces that came after them. Instead, Tor, Drake, and Raine ended up sending a bear after *them*. This made Tor's stiff muscles relax a little in his chair. If anyone was going to be upset, it would have to be the security guys being chased by a crazy sick bear who wanted more of Tor's delicious honey-nut trail bar.

"Now let's get out our study guides. We have a lot to go over before finals." Mrs. Petrus tapped the board with her marker. "We stopped at page four, so let's pick up again there."

*** 

"Look at those." Raine glared at the pallet of water bottles in the cafeteria, each labeled with the soaring black hawk of Thayne Mining. Students had already made a big dent in the pile and more were snatching bottles from the pallet as they got into the lunch line.

"I'm not drinking that." Drake got in line. He wore an orange-and-blue sweater with alien saucer ships knitted all over the front of it. "I sure hope Veggie Girl isn't hungry today. I'm starving."

"Gemma." Tor picked up a tray and put his water bottle on it.

"What?"

"Gemma. We can't call her Veggie Girl now. We know her, you know, outside of school. Her name is Gemma."

"Tor's right." Raine walked with them, her lunch bag in her hand. "We've been to her house. That means we're practically friends."

"Raine's right. You're almost dating." Tor nodded.

Drake threw Tor a horrified glance and then snorted when Tor couldn't hold his serious expression and broke into a grin. "You're rotten."

"No, this is. What is it?" Tor regarded the brownish glop on his plate, which steamed and spread out and smelled a lot like Roscoe's dog food.

"Goulash," the lunch lady said grimly. "We can't use water in the kitchen. So this is from a can."

"From World War Two?" Drake asked, but the lunch lady was already scooping out a serving for him. He watched it plop onto his plate and then they moved down the line, collecting a scoop of canned fruit cocktail, some hard rolls, and a container of milk.

"You really need to start packing lunches." Raine looked at their trays with genuine sympathy. "Wow."

"We won World War Two on this goulash." Tor raised one eyebrow at her. "Right, Drake?"

"Probably because we fed it to the Nazis." Drake wove his way through the tables and seated himself at Veggie Gir—Gemma's table. She looked paler and more upset than ever. Tanya and Marie looked no better.

"Hi Gemma." Tor sat down but there were no crispy chicken nuggets to share. The girls were eating their rolls already, and Drake's shoulders slumped a little when he saw that. The rolls were the only edible part of the meal.

"You can have my goulash," Gemma offered, squinting at him through her glasses. Her plastic barrettes were red again, like little devil horns on each side of her forehead. "Are you feeling okay? How's your hair?"

"My what?" Tor put his hand up to his head, confused. Was there something in his hair?

"His hair isn't falling out. There's nothing wrong with him, Gemma." Raine unwrapped a thick sandwich and took a bite. She spoke through her mouthful of food. "He doesn't have radiation poisoning. Or rabies."

Gemma gave Raine a look of dislike and her two friends joined her, looking as alike as triplets for a moment.

Tor took his hand down from his hair and picked up a roll. He took a bite and chewed and swallowed with an effort. The roll was crumbly and sour tasting. "I'm fine."

"I think these rolls are from a can, too." Drake crumbled his into his goulash.

"They've been testing every water drainage from the mountain ranges around here ever since my dad alerted the feds." Gemma turned her attention back to Tor, her blue eyes worried behind her glasses. "They'll know where it's coming from pretty soon."

"Who's 'they'?" Tor asked. "The Division of Wildlife?"

"No, the EPA, Environmental Protection Agency." Gemma nodded. "The Division of Wildlife calls them in if they think there might be contamination. What?"

Drake, Tor, and Raine exchanged glances.

"The EPA, like that idiot guy in *Ghostbusters* who turns off the power grid?" Tor asked.

"That's a movie, Tor." Gemma clasped her hands together and put them on the table, looking down her nose at them. "The EPA representative has been working with Mayor Malone and my dad."

"And Thayne Mining, I bet." Raine looked over at the shiny pallet of water bottles. The soaring hawk of Thayne Mining was repeated over and over in the hundreds of labels, reflected in the water to make hundreds more.

Drake took a single bite of goulash and spit it out in his napkin. Tor put his own forkful down. Around him he saw untouched goulash on almost every plate.

"Let's dump this and get out of here—" Tor started to get up but sat down again as Principal Crandall appeared in the doorway, holding the battery-powered megaphone he used when he wanted to speak to a crowd. Mr. Crandall's white hair was a thin, downy fuzz around his head and his skin was freckled with age. He used to be tall, and was still taller than most of the kids even though he stooped over a bit now. He always wore a suit, and even though he looked like a breeze could blow him over, he was as tough as granite, a fact that many students at Snow Park Middle/High found out to their regret when they misbehaved. Mr. Crandall turned on the megaphone and cleared his throat to quiet the kids, although a waiting hush had already descended upon the cafeteria.

"Ahem. Yes. The water contamination source has been found and will be corrected as soon as possible. The EPA requests that we keep drinking bottled water for at least six days—" At this a muttering groan swept like a breeze across the seated students, most of them sitting in front of untouched messes of goulash. Mr. Crandall raised his hand and the muttering subsided. "We have had a generous donation of bottled water from Thayne Mining and they'll be supplying pizzas for tomorrow's lunch."

Mr. Crandall paused again, this time for the cheers. Tor didn't cheer, and neither did anyone at his table. He knew something bad was coming; he knew it like he knew heavy snow was coming, the way the air tasted electric and his skin tingled. A phrase from Mrs. Petrus's study guide leaped into his mind, the quote from the witches in *Macbeth*: "By the pricking of my thumbs, something wicked this way comes."

"Thanks for your patience, students." He put down the megaphone and stepped over to their table. "Raine, can you come to the front office, please?"

Eyes turned to her. Raine looked surprised for a flicker of a second and then her expression shut down as if she'd dropped shutters over herself. She nodded and placed the remains of her lunch in her bag as the cafeteria erupted with whispers and then louder chatter. Tor's face burned with heat and as she stood up, he stood up with her, and so did Drake.

"Don't." Raine put her hand out. "They only asked for me."

"Well, they got all of us," Tor said. "Always. Right?"

"Right." Drake picked up his tray and tossed his bangs back from his eyelashes. "See you, Gemma. Tanya. Marie."

Gemma stared at him behind her glasses, her barrettes perfectly level at each side of her head, but Tanya and Marie both melted into sappy grins. Tor picked up his tray and followed Drake and Raine, feeling the greedy gaze of every kid in school crawling over him, the whispers following them.

Raine marched out of the cafeteria and they set their trays on the disposal counter and followed, walking together to the principal's office where Mr. Crandall waited, a sympathetic expression on his wrinkled face.

"Your friends don't need to be here." Mr. Crandall sat down behind his desk. "This concerns you, Raine."

Tor opened his mouth to speak, but Raine put up her hand in a gesture and he fell silent.

"Is it my dad?" Raine asked in a tiny whisper, and for a second her stone face cracked and Tor saw her terror. "My mom? Grandmother?"

"Oh, no, not at all." Mr. Crandall patted his desk as though he was trying to pat Raine's hands, which were clenched at her sides. "Your family is fine—well—"

"What?" Drake said impatiently.

"The source of the contamination is from your family's property, from Borsh Mountain." Mr. Crandall blinked and looked down at his desk as though he didn't want to look at Raine's expression. "The EPA determined that it's coming from your land. Your family requested that you come home. They're having a meeting with the mayor and the town board. And the EPA. There might be a lawsuit filed against your family."

The world went roaring away from Tor. The mountain lion on Borsh Mountain, sick and dying. The bear, attacking the log. There was evil in the town, all right, and it had made a home on Raine's family land.

"No, boys, you don't get to go with her." Mr. Crandall stood up behind his desk as Drake and Tor started to follow Raine, who headed for the door without another word.

"What? But we're—" Tor started.

"Going back to class." Mr. Crandall clapped his hands together. "You can meet your friend after school, if she wants to see you."

"But Raine—" Drake started.

Raine turned at the door, her face calm, her lips held tight together so they wouldn't tremble. "I'll be okay. I have—I have to get home. See you later."

Then she was gone, and Mr. Crandall's thin hands came down on their shoulders and gave a gentle squeeze. "It's okay, boys. I know you're anxious. We all are. Just try to get your schoolwork done so you pass finals. You don't want to repeat the ninth grade."

"Yes, sir," Tor mumbled, still wondering if he could make a break for the exit. Sure he could. Then what?

"Let's get back to class." Drake shrugged his backpack higher onto his shoulder, dislodging Mr. Crandall's hand. "We'll be late if we don't go."

"Thanks, Tor, Drake." Mr. Crandall returned to his desk and sat down slowly, settling into his chair with a sigh and a creak of old wood. "I appreciate your maturity."

"Maturity." Drake nearly spat the word as they hurried down the hall. "I'd like to show that old guy some maturity." He clenched his hand into a fist.

"Oh, stop it. It isn't his fault. Meet me right after school," Tor said. "We've got to get geared up. We'll try to get Raine to come along but if we can't—"

"Then what? Where are we going—oh." Drake nodded thoughtfully as they reached Tor's science classroom door. "Right."

There were three people in the world who knew every inch of Raine's mountain, and two of them were standing right here. They had to find out what was poisoning the land. They were going to take the chairlift to the highest peak after school and snowboard into Borsh Mountain.

# Chapter Fourteen

## Losing the Mountain

"Tor, wait!" Gemma called out. Tor slowed, but he didn't stop walking as she hurried to catch up to him. The longest school day he'd ever endured was over, and if she thought he was going to hang around one moment longer in the gloomy halls of Snow Park Middle/High School, she was crazy. She caught up to him and he scowled at her.

"What?"

Gemma frowned back at him. "Don't bark at me." She wore a black wool pea coat and clutched her hat and gloves in one hand.

"I'm in a hurry, Gemma. Can't it wait?"

"I know what you're going to do." She plucked at his sleeve with pale fingers. "I know where you came from when you found that mountain lion—"

Tor spun around to her and she took a step back. "You don't know anything!"

She put her fists on her hips. "Actually, I do. And I don't think you should—"

"What are you going to do, Gemma?" Drake appeared at her other side, flipping his bangs back from his blue eyes, giving her a sunny smile that would have turned Gemma's friends into puddles. "Turn us in? We're just going snowboarding."

"You're going—I know what you're going to do. It's dangerous." Gemma's eyes looked watery behind her glasses and her face was paler than ever. "You just can't."

"Well, we're going to. Let's go, Drake." Tor pulled away from her grip and kept walking, speeding up. He glanced back to see Gemma standing still in the hallway, clutching her gloves in her hands. Tor turned and hit the school doors with both hands and burst into the outside, the fresh air filling his lungs. The day was cold again, threatening snow, but with the wet feeling of spring. The snowflakes that spiraled out of the sky were huge, slushy, melting immediately as soon as they hit the pavement. The snow would be soft and sticky under their boards, tough to move through.

Drake pulled his knit cap over his hair and tucked his bangs out of the way. "I'll meet you at Raine's."

"I have to feed Roscoe and leave a note for my mom." Tor was jogging now, his breath puffing out in clouds around his head.

"Don't tell your mom we're going up there," Drake warned him.

"She knows everything anyway," Tor said.

Drake smacked him on the arm. "Just don't. She'll stop us."

Tor shrugged. "Fine. I won't tell her." He raised a hand as Drake headed toward the condominiums near the slopes where his dad kept his bachelor pad and held all his wild parties, and where Drake stored his snowboarding gear. Tor had offered to let Drake keep his gear at Tor's house, but Drake told Tor that if he didn't keep his snowboard there his dad would think he'd moved out. Drake said this with a laugh and a toss of his hair, but his eyes didn't smile along with his mouth. Tor didn't ask again. He continued toward home where Roscoe was waiting, his enormous head peering over the fence to see if he could spot his boy, his tail wagging anxiously.

"Hi, Roscoe." Tor took a moment to ruffle his dog's head and let him dance around his legs. Roscoe shoved into him so hard he nearly fell over. "Let's get you fed. I have to go snowboarding."

*Lying to your dog?* Raine's voice said in his head. *That's a bad sign, Tor.*

"Why does my conscience sound like Raine?" Tor asked Roscoe, who wagged his tail harder. "Okay. I'm going onto Borsh Mountain to find whatever it is that's poisoning the water, and you can't come with me. Dogs can't snowboard."

Roscoe's tail stopped wagging and he regarded Tor with his wise, black-lined eyes, tilting his head as though he were trying to puzzle out exactly what Tor was talking about.

"Come on, boy." Tor sprang up the porch steps and unlocked the door. He hurried to the kitchen and fed Roscoe quickly, then packed his snowboarding pack with food, bottled water, flashlights, Mr. Douglas's nifty emergency kit that they all carried with them, and a length of climber's rope that his mom gave him for Christmas this year. She'd also given him a coupon for a climbing class this coming summer. She was a great mom.

He hesitated. She *was* a great mom. Lying to her was wrong. But they'd be deep on Borsh Mountain when she got home, right? She wouldn't be able to stop them if he left her a note. He picked up the marker to write on the board where they left messages for each other.

*Gone to snowboard and see our friends up high,* he wrote. *You know. Back before dark.* There. She would know what that meant.

"I'll be back soon," he said to Roscoe, closing his dog into the garage with its heated bed and a dog door to the yard. Roscoe gave a sigh and scrambled into his bed right away, used to his boy going snowboarding after school. He gave Tor a look that clearly meant *I like summer better.*

Tor gave him a quick rub of the ears, then grabbed his snowboard and helmet. Drake would be waiting for him already. He stomped into his boots and zipped up his snowboarding jacket and shouldered out the door, carrying his helmet and snowboard. He trotted down to Main

Street, expecting to see Drake standing out front of Raine's building, but Drake was nowhere to be seen.

The Pro Shop was dark, which never happened. Raine's family lived right above their sports rental business and Mr. Douglas or one of the family members was always behind the counter. The "Closed" sign gave Tor an unhappy sensation in his stomach. He usually went inside the shop and put his snowboard in the rack by the door before going upstairs to see Raine in the family's apartment, but now there was no place to put his board. He hesitated, then rang the bell by the private entrance, a door that led to a set of stairs up to the second floor.

He shuffled back and forth in his boots, feeling time draining away, big snowflakes spiraling out of the sky and landing on his jacket with wet plops, his nose starting to run in the cold. The door opened abruptly and he nearly jumped out of his boots as Grandmother Douglas appeared. She wore soft black trousers and a heavy, dark green sweater, and her hair, long and thick as Raine's but snow-white, lay in a single braid over her shoulder. Her wrinkled face stared at him with a stony expression that shifted into a tiny expression of relief.

"Tor." She looked beyond his shoulder and nodded. "Drake."

Tor turned to see Drake trotting up. Drake skidded to a stop, his breath puffing white clouds into the steel-gray afternoon air, his cheeks pink. "Hi, Grandmother."

Grandmother Douglas turned her fierce, bird-like glare from Tor to Drake. She nodded and gestured for them to come into the small landing at the foot of the stairs. She shut the door behind them as they shuffled in. She stepped up onto the stairs as Drake set his board against one wall and Tor set his against the other one, which left them just enough room to stand with their shoulders touching. A single bulb inside a frosted glass gave a wan bit of light. Grandmother turned to call up: "Raine. Your friends are here."

"We—" Tor began, and stopped as Raine came down the stairs as silently as the library ghost. She wore jeans and a sweatshirt, her mocassined feet making no sound, her face pale and shadowed. She saw them and started to say something when Grandmother Douglas put up her hand. She stopped. Above them, inside the apartment, Tor could hear deep voices and light voices talking together and sometimes over one another. None of the voices sounded happy.

"Tor, give me your hand." Grandmother Douglas held out her palm and Tor put it in hers immediately. She peeled back his glove and examined his wrist, covered now with a small bandage. She didn't take the bandage off but looked at it closely and then gave it a sniff. She nodded and pulled his sleeve back down and turned to her granddaughter.

"I must ask you to act in my place, Raine." She stepped up the stair and took Raine's hand in hers. Raine put out her other hand and caught her grandmother's frail hand in both of hers.

"Grandmother?" she whispered.

"I am too old to walk our mountain anymore." Grandmother sighed. "I wish it weren't so. But you three have explored every tree, climbed every rock, just as I did when I was a girl."

"We're not allowed to—" Tor started, and then stopped and dropped his gaze. He couldn't lie to Grandmother. She was right. In the winters they snowboarded to the valley to visit the otters in their winter playground, and in the summer they'd explored all over the dangerous Borsh Mountain, with its unmarked mine shafts and deep, hidden pits. They blazed trees around each pit they found and added it to a secret map that Raine kept locked in her room.

They didn't explore inside the mine shafts. Tor ended up in one to escape an avalanche once and he'd nearly died. Borsh Mountain really was a death trap, but it was Raine's family land and it was filled with wildlife and it was all theirs, no one else's, and Tor loved it.

Now something had come along to live in it. Tor's heart burned in his chest and he shifted in his snowboarding boots, ready to go, to run, to *do* something.

"You must find what is wrong with our mountain," Grandmother Douglas said. "Your father would go, but the mayor is already speaking of a lawsuit. You know what this will mean."

Raine nodded, her lips pressed together tightly. Tor glanced up the stairs where the Douglas family lived. They weren't poor, but they weren't rich either. If the mayor filed a big lawsuit, the Douglas family would be forced to—

"The mayor. He'll make them sell Borsh Mountain," Tor whispered. "He's wanted it forever."

Drake made a hissing sound through his teeth. "His company will turn it into another ski mountain."

"They wish to take it." Grandmother Douglas nodded. "You three are the only ones who know our land as I do, as my son does."

Raine nodded, her face pale in the wan light.

"Your father must stay here, Raine. You three must go. Be careful. Come back at full dark and tell me what you find."

"Yes, ma'am," Drake said quietly. Tor nodded.

Grandmother Douglas regarded them all and then nodded. She started up the stairs, still holding Raine's hand, tugging her along. "You're just a child," she said loudly, imperiously. "You mustn't be around this discussion. This is for the adults." Another step. "You need fresh air." Step. "And exercise." Step. "And to get away from this trouble."

Grandmother Douglas disappeared into the family apartment and a moment later so did Raine. Tor and Drake stood in the stuffy landing, waiting. Tor unzipped his jacket so he wouldn't start to sweat in the warmth.

"Come on, Raine," Tor muttered.

"Listen," Drake said, tilting his ear to the stairs. Above them, voices quarreled, and then Grandmother Douglas's bright, high voice pierced the air, commandingly. The conversation hushed, then began again. Raine appeared, her snowboard in her hands, her jacket unzipped and her helmet unsnapped. Her untied snowboard boots rattled as she hurried down the stairs.

"Quick." She made pushing gestures with her hands. "Before Mom and Dad change their minds."

Tor opened the door and they burst out into a world filled with wet snowflakes and gray skies. The door slammed behind them. Raine tied her boots quickly and they were on their way, Raine buckling her helmet and zipping her jacket as they hurried down Main Street towards the chairlifts.

"We only have three hours before dark." Drake looked into the sky. "Maybe less if this storm gets heavier."

"That's not much time." Tor led the way through the streets, though the Snow Park lodge, and onto the packed slopes where the chairlift hummed and rattled. The crowds were already thinning but lots of town kids were taking advantage of the last snowboarding and skiing of the day, perhaps the whole season.

Tor saw faces turn toward them and then away, buzzing and whispering to each other. Raine put her stone face on as they stood in line to get on the chairlift. Drake tossed his mane of hair back and settled his helmet on his head with flamboyant gestures. He pulled on his gloves and snapped his foot into his snowboard bindings, and Tor couldn't help grinning at his goofy friend. When you were an outcast, it helped when your fellow outcast was as good-looking as a movie star.

Tor snapped into his board, admiring the decoration of a glowing ocean sunset with a single dark shark's fin, and the three long scratches left by the mountain lion. Best snowboard ever. The three of them showed their passes to the chairlift attendant, who glared at them as if they were serial killers. Tor ignored him as they slid forward and settled into the chairlift. The chair swept up and out and they were free, traveling into the mountain air with no one around but them. Tor sighed.

"Back to the days when everybody hated me. Feels like old times." He swung his snowboard back and forth gently as the lift took them up the mountain. Snowflakes continued to spiral out of the sky, but as they rose, the flakes became smaller and thicker, piling up on their helmets and the shoulders of their jackets.

"People are stupid." Drake put his chin up and looked down at his nose at the people skiing and snowboarding below them. "They'll believe anything."

"Anything bad about my people," Raine said in a low voice. Drake was between the two of them so Tor couldn't reach out and pat her shoulder. Drake didn't pat her. He gave her a scornful look.

"Oh, please, I'm white and people believe all sorts of bad things about me. If someone told them I was shooting meth or drinking heroin, they'd totally believe it."

"It's taking meth or shooting heroin, you idiot." Raine smiled a little bit.

"And Tor, look at him. Everyone believes he's a total blockhead. Of course that's 'cause he looks like one, but—ow." Drake rubbed his arm and gave a mock glare at Tor.

"We'll get this sorted out, Raine." Tor settled his helmet on his head more firmly and zipped his jacket up to the neck. The temperature dropped rapidly and the snow came harder, blowing ribbons across the slopes below them and swirling around the chairlift.

"I like the snow. No one will see us disappear." Drake worked his hands deeper into his gloves as the end of the chairlift approached. "Let's roll."

# Chapter Fifteen

## Poison

The spring snow felt like sand under Tor's snowboard, thick and soft and slow. Snowflakes swirled around them as Drake dodged under the boundary fence and onto Borsh Mountain. Raine followed, and Tor took a final glance around to see if anyone could see them.

The slopes were deserted in the gray afternoon light. A few skiers had taken the upper mountain chairlift with them, but they'd flown down the slopes while the three were still clicking into their boards.

Good. Tor ducked under the tape that separated the resort from Borsh Mountain and followed Drake and Raine's track through the snow. Raine followed the tiny blazes they'd made on the trees to mark the trail. The falling snow tapered off as they rode across the slope and when they reached the valley Tor could see all the way across. Raine stopped at the edge of the ridge but instead of sitting down she stood poised on her board, her head up and her gaze turning up and down the valley. Drake stopped next to her, his breath puffing out in clouds around his head.

"See anything?" Tor slid up next to Drake, his breath coming a little faster than it should. This was exactly where the mountain lion jumped him and slashed his wrist. Did the mountain lion have a mate, as sick as he was, licking her chops and looking at them right now? Tor scanned the woods around them, seeing nothing but snow and dark green pines.

"The otters are out." Raine unfastened her boots from her snowboard and sat on it like a surfboard, her knees up, her eyes shining. "Look."

In the valley below them, a sleek dark shape climbed out of the river and waddled up the bank. Another one followed, then another. Two of them started wrestling and, as they played, the third one leaped over them and slid down toward the river in an icy channel like a sledding run. The otter's paws waved wildly as it disappeared into the dark water with a splash. The other wrestling otters fell into the channel and slid down together, squeaking happily, and shot into the water. Their noses came out of the river and the three stayed together, heads touching, looking like they were talking, exactly like Tor, Drake, and Raine would stand together to talk on the slopes.

Tor unlatched his boots from his snowboard and sat down, eyes on the swimming otters. "They look healthy."

"They look great. You know what that means, right?" Raine rubbed her gloved hands together.

"Sure! Okay, no," Drake said.

"Nope." Tor looked over at Drake and shrugged.

"It means the source of the poison is below this valley, this watershed. That narrows it down a lot." Raine dug into the front of her parka and brought out their secret map. Tor leaned over to see and Drake shuffled around to the other side of Raine so they could all peer at the waterproof map together.

"Look." Raine's finger traced the otter's river valley down towards Snow Park. "This is the main water drainage towards town."

"But the mountain lion was all the way up here," Tor objected. "How did he get sick if the poison wasn't in this valley?"

Drake reached out and smacked Tor on the back of his helmet. "Lions roam, dummy."

"Oh, right." Tor rubbed the back of his helmet. "So he could have drunk poisoned water down below us, and then come up here to hunt the otters."

"And the other drainages from Borsh Mountain go away from town, not towards it." Raine drew her finger along the pale blue lines of creeks that joined into bigger creeks and finally into bigger and bigger rivers that became, eventually, the Colorado River. "All the mountains give their water to the rivers and to the sea. One side flows to the Atlantic, one side to the Pacific."

"That's the Continental Divide, right?" Tor kept an eye on the otters as they scrambled out of the river and raced back to the top of their sledding hill. If the animals disappeared or became alarmed, they'd know danger was coming.

"Exactly. We're on the Pacific side here, so all water drains west, eventually. And I'm betting our poison starts right about here." Raine put her finger on the map, where they'd marked a double X. Tor remembered that place from the past summer, a rusted metal gate that sealed up the mouth of a tunnel barely wide enough to stand up in. He leaned in to look closer, the falling snow speckling the waterproof paper and making round dots of water. His stomach started fizzing with excitement. "That's close to a stream, right?"

"Right." Drake clapped his hands together and at the sound the otters all paused at the top of their sledding hill and stood up on their hind legs, their front paws folded against their stomachs, their doglike faces peering up at the ridge. Tor, Drake and Raine froze, staying silent so the otters wouldn't leave.

This time it didn't work. One otter gave a chirp that sounded like he was more disgusted than scared, and he slid down the riverbank, splashed into the water, and disappeared. His friends followed, and in a few moments, the valley felt deserted.

"Sorry." Drake clenched his gloved hands. "I forgot to be quiet."

"It's okay," Tor said. "We need to get going. There's not much day-light left. Let's get to that mine shaft and see if there's anything—"

"Glowing? Green, and glowing?" Raine scrambled to her feet and clicked her boots into her snowboard. She settled her helmet on her head as if she were going into battle. Her eyes flashed in the gray after-noon light.

"Exactly. Time to finish this." Tor stood up and clicked into his own snowboard, his heart starting to hurry up in his chest. "We're going to find that poison and that ghost."

Raine looked at their secret valley, pine trees on every side, the dark water of the river chuckling through the snow, the otters warm and safe in their earthen den below the earth, and she raised her hand solemnly.

"We will find what killed you, big brother. We will find it." She put her hand to her heart and so did Drake and Tor. Things that seemed stupid and silly in town, things that Tor wouldn't be caught dead doing with other people around, weren't stupid at all when it was just the three of them in the forest. Tor thought of the mountain lion, so beau-tiful and so deadly, starved thin and sick. They were going to find that poison, and they were going to find out what the glowing green thing that haunted them wanted. They were going to put it all right again.

"This way." Raine hopped on her board and sent it carving a path through the trackless snow. "Follow me. And quiet!"

Tor bent his knees and hopped, and his board came alive under his feet, sliding into the channel left by Raine's board. Behind him Drake gave a little huff of excitement and they were off through the trees. The slope was steep and filled with standing trees and downed timber, so Raine took a slow, lateral track across the mountainside, heading left and then right in a long S-shape. This kept them from going too fast and they could scan down through the trees as they slid sideways. Tor's leg muscles started to burn with the effort of holding himself along the slope and he forced himself to relax, to give in to the movement of his board.

Tor couldn't see anything but more trees and more snow, and he focused on following Raine as she glided down the mountainside. His breath came faster as Raine finally stopped behind a tree. She leaned down to unhook one boot from her board. They were here. Tor peered down through the trees.

"It's hard to tell but I think it's right there." Raine pointed. A moment later Tor saw a black opening in the side of the slope.

"That's it," Drake breathed. He leaned down and unhooked both his boots from the board. "Come on, let's go."

Tor unsnapped his other boot. They set their snowboards next to each other against a tree. Tor thought uneasily that if they didn't hurry, they'd lose the last of the daylight. The black opening in front of them wasn't the only mine opening on Borsh Mountain. To stay after dark would be really stupid.

"Slow and careful." Raine pulled on Tor's sleeve as he started forward. "Slow."

"Okay." Tor stepped forward, sinking up to his knees in the deep snow that they'd glided over coming down on their snowboards. He strode forward, his breath puffing. Drake followed in Tor's footsteps and Raine followed him. Tor reached the rusted metal gate that blocked the mine entrance and stopped, panting, sweating despite the cold. He threw a glance back at Drake and Raine, a few steps behind him.

"Is there anything there?" Raine's cheeks were pink with cold, her black eyes fierce with hope. Tor shook his head. All this way, and there was nothing there.

"Nothing." He reached out and kicked the metal grid that made the gate. "There's nothing—" He stopped in amazement as the gate shivered and swung open with a zinging sound.

"Someone's been in here." Raine touched the fence. "There was an old padlock on it this summer."

Drake reached back to his daypack and pulled out his cell phone. "No coverage. There's never any up here."

"This is the source of the poison." Raine stepped into the entrance and stared into the long tunnel going into blackness. "I can tell."

"How?"

"Look." Raine pointed. Tor shuffled around until he stood right next to her, and he took a sharp intake of breath. He gestured for Drake to join them.

"What is it—oh."

The three of them stood in the entrance, looking at a faint green glow far away from them, down the tunnel that was carved into the mountain.

They'd found their poison.

# Chapter Sixteen

## A Cavern of Secrets

Raine didn't make a sound as she walked into the mine, even though she wore clunky snowboarding boots instead of her usual moccasins. It just wasn't fair. Tor tried to follow just as silently, but his boots crunched in the icy gravel that covered the ground inside the tunnel. His breath puffed out in a cloud around his head. The inside of the mineshaft felt even colder than the outside. Tor missed Roscoe's big shaggy bulk and his excellent dog nose. Roscoe would know what was making that green glow.

Tor knew it wasn't radiation. He'd read about radiation after the mountain lion had attacked him. Radiation didn't make you glow green. It didn't smell bad or look bad. It just killed you in the worst possible way, by shooting invisible gamma rays through your body and destroying you from the inside until you lost your hair and puked up your insides. Radiation was not what was causing the glow, it couldn't be. But what was it? The light increased steadily as they walked deeper into the tunnel.

Raine held up a hand and Tor froze. Her hand glimmered in the green light. Drake put his hand on Tor's shoulder and the weight of his friend's hand steadied him.

"Quiet." Raine breathed the word softly. Her breath drifted like smoke from her mouth. Tor could hear something ahead of them now, and what he heard couldn't be real, could it?

Someone was singing. Raine ghosted forward and Tor followed and the tune started sounding familiar.

"She'll be coming round the mountain when she comes…"

The green glow became stronger, painting the walls and floor with dim light, exposing rocks and ancient timbers that braced the walls and ceiling. A rotten timber lay on the floor in front of them, half-buried in rocks and dirt. Tor glanced at the ceiling and wished he hadn't. The place where the timber had fallen was packed with jumbled rocks that looked as though they could all come down at a sneeze. They shouldn't be in here.

"She'll be coming round the mountain…." The voice was low, male, and familiar. Tor tilted his head to the side like Roscoe did when he was puzzled, trying to hear harder. Who was that?

Raine twirled her hand for them to follow and stepped carefully over the debris and the downed timber, lifting her foot high in the air like a cartoon character. Tor waited until she was over and then followed. His boot slipped on the powdery dirt with a gritting sound and he froze, heart pounding, waiting for a shout of discovery. They stood like statues, not moving, their breath curling around their heads.

"Coming around the mountain, she'll be—what was it? " The man stopped for a moment, then began singing the first part of the song again. "She'll be coming round the mountain…"

Tor finished stepping over the downed timber. Drake followed without a misstep. Ahead of them, the tunnel abruptly turned to the left. The glow became brighter, light enough to see Raine's expression when she turned back to them.

She mouthed the words at them. "What do we do?"

Tor put his hands up and pretended he was looking around the corner. Beside him, Drake nodded. He then leaned down and picked up a baseball-sized rock from the rough ground. Tor crouched and picked one up too, his hands clumsy from the cold. Even though he was in his snowboarding gear and had his best winter gloves on, the cold was creeping in. His nose was freezing and his toes were numb.

Raine nodded, her mouth a thin line, her eyes squinted down into deadly triangles. She made the follow-me gesture again and turned back around.

"She'll be—doing something," the man sang, and they poked their heads around the corner.

Tor couldn't get his mind around the scene in front of them. He knew he was looking at dozens of green glow sticks scattered everywhere in a large, hollowed-out space, but what were those barrels? There were hundreds of them, each one big enough to hold a full-grown person, a color that probably looked blue in the daylight but were a swampy green in the light of the sticks. Stickers were plastered all over the barrels, and Drake tensed at Tor's shoulder. The stickers were hawks, over and over again—the soaring black hawk of Thayne Mining.

A man popped up behind the barrels, his handsome face smiling and his mouth open in song.

"Coming round the mountain... Oh. Hi. Just saw you, there." Mr. Stanley, the town handyman, wearing coveralls, work boots, and a dark woolen cap, gave them a little wave with the crowbar he held in his hand.

"What—what are you doing?" Tor asked.

"I'm trying to seal up these barrels, of course." Mr. Stanley gestured around him. "They're leaking. That's what's causing the groundwater contamination. Chemicals. Mercury. You know, stuff like that."

"How did you find this place? How did you know?" Raine stepped out and Drake drifted out behind Tor, keeping back a few steps.

Mr. Stanley gave them a rueful grin. "I put them here, of course. I thought they would stay sealed for a thousand years. Stupid thousand-year barrels didn't even last five years." He laughed. Tor, Raine, and Drake didn't join in.

"You put them here." Raine made a tiny gesture at the earth below her feet, her ground, her family ground, as sacred to her as a church. Tor's fist trembled as his grip tightened around the rock he held behind his back. Mr. Stanley made a shrugging gesture with the crowbar.

"Look, it wasn't supposed to be this way." He waved at the barrels around them. "These are from Thayne Mining. In order to get molybdenum processed, the company creates some nasty byproducts. Arsenic. Mercury. Sulfuric acid—oh, hey, that's what happened with this one." He squatted down to look at the base of a barrel. Tor could see a brown substance darkening the bottom edge of the barrel and a dribble of something staining the dirt around it. His toes curled up in his boots as he saw the stain disappearing under another barrel with different markings on it.

"That's sulfuric acid?" Raine pointed.

"Quite a few of these are. It's caustic like you wouldn't believe, and it's contaminated with all sorts of nasty stuff from the processing." Mr. Stanley wiped a hand over his brow. "I'm sure glad you're here. This is a big job. It'll be good to get your help."

"You're glad we're here?" Tor asked. Happy Mr. Stanley, town handyman, was acting like it was no big deal that he stood in the midst of a toxic waste dump. "Why—you want us to help?"

"Don't you want to?" Mr. Stanley frowned at them. "This is what's making the water bad. We can't stop this until we get these barrels sealed up again."

"Mr. Stanley," Tor said patiently. "We need to tell the town. We need to get these barrels out of here—"

"No!" Mr. Stanley shouted so loudly that something rumbled and trembled in the distance, and then let go with a crash that almost shook them off their feet. Tor turned around. A tiny circle of dim daylight still showed behind them. A timber must have fallen in another tunnel, not the one that led to the exit.

"Mr. Stanley." Tor made soothing gestures with his hands. Drake remained quiet behind him, standing in the shadows, compact and tense. Raine, too, fell silent.

"That was scary." Mr. Stanley peered down a side tunnel that was barely visible behind stacks of barrels. "I think this place is haunted sometimes. I hear things. Voices. That's why I sing, to keep them out of my head. To keep them away."

"Why can't we get the barrels out of here?" Tor asked quietly.

"Because I got paid to take them to the hazardous waste disposal site, and if anyone finds out that I took the money and stashed the barrels here instead, and that's what's been making everything sick, then that's not going to be good, is it? Is it?"

"No, it's not," Tor agreed. "That wouldn't be good at all." He felt like he might just throw up on his snowboard boots. Mr. Stanley grinned at them, his eyes glowing in the dim light.

"Right! Let's get working, then, okay? These chemlights I bought from old Mr. Galloway won't last for more than a few hours."

"Chemlights?" Tor asked.

Mr. Stanley waved a hand at the glowsticks. "Army surplus. Green so they don't spoil night vision, who cares about that, but there's no chance of a flame. Wouldn't be good, heh."

"Right," Tor said through numb lips. A hissing Coleman lantern would cause a giant explosion. No wonder Mr. Stanley was working in the dim light.

"We need to slide this new sheeting under these barrels and tie it up tight. That should last a hundred years at least," Mr. Stanley said, and made come-on gestures at them.

"Sure, Mr. Stanley." Tor put on his friendliest smile and stepped out into the cavern. "We'll help you." He prayed Raine wasn't going to jump at Mr. Stanley and claw his eyes out. The handyman was a lot bigger then they were and he had a crowbar, besides.

After a long pause, enough that Tor's smile muscles started to tremble, Raine stepped up to his shoulder.

"Sure, Mr. Stanley." Her voice cracked a little bit. The glowsticks painted her face a sickly green. She waved at a barrel. "How do we get this wrapped up?"

"It's easy." Mr. Stanley leaned down and came up with a roll of plastic sheeting, the end flapping free. "We have to lever the barrel up so I can get the sheeting underneath it. Here, Tor, you push on this barrel. Raine, come stand by me."

It all happened so fast. Raine stepped up to Mr. Stanley and he seized her around her middle, pinning her arms to her sides and pulling her against him.

"Raine!" Tor stepped forward. Raine smashed the back of her helmeted head against Mr. Stanley's face and he bellowed in pain. He lifted Raine off her feet as she kicked at his shins with the heels of her boots. She cried out as Mr. Stanley jabbed the crowbar up under her chin. She stopped kicking.

"One more step and I'll crush her throat." Mr. Stanley's smile was gone, his eyes as flat and dead as a snake's. His nose dribbled blood down to his chin, black in the dim light of the cavern. "You think I couldn't tell you were trying to fool me?"

"We're not fooling you, Mr. Stanley." Tor put both his hands out, his palms up and wide open. "We want to help."

"You can't turn me in. I can fix this. Nobody has to know." He made a gesture with his chin at Drake. "Go over and sit next to that barrel, Drake. You too, Tor. I don't want to hurt her, but I will."

Drake moved out of the shadows and to the barrel, his eyes glinting in the green light, his mouth compressed to a furious line. Tor walked stiffly over to join Drake.

"Don't hurt her." Drake ordered, and then plopped down. Tor sat next to him. The cold seeped into him through the seat of his pants, making him even colder than before. He started shivering.

"You stay there." Mr. Stanley moved into the tunnel that they'd just come through, dragging Raine with him. Her feet scrabbled in the dirt and kicked up small stones. Her hands tugged at his arms around her, her chin raised up as the crowbar dug into her soft skin. "Stay there!"

Tor jumped to his feet as soon as Mr. Stanley was a dozen feet down the tunnel and Drake followed. Mr. Stanley yanked Raine along, stumbling over the fallen timber and regaining his feet. The daylight at the entrance seemed like noon after the dark of the mine. The handyman released Raine and shoved her down the tunnel at them, and as Raine fell into their arms, he slammed the gate shut and tucked his crowbar under his arm. He snatched a padlock from his jacket and locked the gate.

They were trapped inside.

# Chapter Seventeen

## The Ghost Without a Face

"I just need time to think." Mr. Stanley clutched his head and paced back and forth at the entrance to the tunnel. The dying day behind him was as gray as ashes. His breath puffed around his head.

"You have to let us go." Tor rattled the metal gate and kicked it. "You can't keep us locked up here!"

Mr. Stanley whirled and leaped at the gate, pressing his face inches from Tor. Tor stumbled back. The man's eyes were bloodshot, his teeth bared. His breath smelled terrible, bitter, as if he'd been drinking gasoline. "I need to think!"

His shout brought another rumble deep in the earth, followed by a crash of something so heavy it made the ground tremble again. Mr. Stanley let go of the metal and stepped away, his eyes wide. A drift of dirt, like smoke, curled over their heads and out into the fast-dimming light.

"Let us out." Raine clenched her gloved hands together.

Mr. Stanley shook his head. "I'll be back." He turned away and waded through the snow, clutching his head with his hands and then waving them around as if he were talking to someone. Tor pressed his helmet against the metal gate until he couldn't see the handyman anymore, until he could see nothing but tall pines and endless snow.

"He's totally crazy." Drake crouched down on the floor and folded his arms. "And we're going to freeze."

"We have our emergency kits. If we could find wood—" Tor started, and then stopped. The green glow down inside the tunnel was dimmer now, but still visible. "That stuff would explode if we lit a match, wouldn't it?"

"I think it might." Raine crouched down next to Drake and settled in next to him. She patted her hand next to her and Tor squatted down too. They huddled together for a few minutes, not speaking, their breath slowing. Mr. Stanley was gone. The trees outside the chain-link gate grew darker as the last of the daylight started to fade. Snow sifted out of the sky. Tor thought hard.

"We can't break out," he said finally. "Right?"

"Not a chance." Drake reached out with a gloved fist and banged on the gate. "Solid." He grew thoughtful at that and pulled his backpack off. He started rummaging around and Tor expected him to pull out a candy bar, but he didn't take out any food. He made an a-ha sound, then settled back and zipped up his backpack without explaining.

"We can ambush him." Raine folded her arms more firmly around herself. "He'll be back to kill us, I bet. We'll set up a trap. I'll be the bait, you bash his head in with a rock."

"Simple. Brutal. I like it." Drake nodded at Tor. "Where do we set it up?"

"I don't think that'll work," Tor said slowly. "I think he's going to realize there's only one way out of this."

"Killing us. Right. So we kill him." Raine reached up and took one of her braids where it was tucked into her coat, slipping it free so she could hold it in one of her mittened hands. She tugged at it. "Kill or be killed."

"That's the problem." Tor rubbed his gloves together to try to get some feeling back into his fingers. "If we disappear, there's going to be a big search party for us. Grandmother Douglas knows where we went. They'll comb this entire mountain until they find us."

"That won't help us if Mr. Stanley kills us. We'll still be dead." Drake hugged his arms around his backpack.

"So will he, if we're found. And when we're found, so will the mine, and the chemicals. He'll lose everything anyway. I think he's eventually going to realize there's only one way out of this." Tor swallowed hard.

Raine shot to her feet, her braid still clutched in her hands. "He's going to collapse the mine with us inside."

Tor got up. He nodded. "He'll hide the evidence and our bodies at the same time."

Drake scrambled to his feet too. Tor put one arm around Drake and the other around Raine. Raine reached for Drake and pulled him closer so they stood face to face in a dense little triangle. That was better. Their breath mingled and drifted up, and Tor caught a faint smell of garlic from Raine, the scent that bothered him so much a few days ago. He thought of Mrs. Douglas's kitchen and her simmering pots of Italian food. She'd be worried now that it was dark outside. His mom would be, too. He tried to keep panic from taking over his thoughts.

"But if he closes up the mine, the groundwater will still be contaminated. The drums are still going to be in here, leaking." Raine made a gulping sound like she was going to throw up. Tor couldn't see her expression. The dark of the winter night had come upon them.

"I think that's why he left." Tor looked down, even though his friends couldn't see his face. He didn't want them to see how scared he was. "He has to work himself up to kill us."

"And once he figures out that he has to collapse the mine to get away with this, he's got to go find some explosive or something." Drake hissed through his teeth. "We have to get out."

"We have to save the land, the town, the people," Raine whispered. "Whatever happens to us, we can't let him poison everything. The deer. The otters—what, Tor?"

Tor let go of Drake and Raine and clutched his helmeted head in his hands. "I think I have an idea."

"Oh, boy." Drake came out with a shaky laugh. "I don't know whether to be relieved or scared."

"I think you should be scared, mostly." Tor fished his flashlight out of his pack and turned it on. In the spear of light his friend's faces appeared, wan and smeared with dirt, noses pink with cold. He spoke in a whisper, just in case their ideas were wrong and Mr. Stanley was still close by after all. "Raine, where's our map of Borsh Mountain?"

She fumbled in her coat and pulled it out. Tor snatched it and crouched down to spread it on the dirt, his hands trembling. He handed the flashlight to Drake, who aimed it at the map.

"Here's where we are." He pointed at the X that they'd placed to identify the mine entrance. Tiny X's dotted the mountain, each of them marking a tunnel or shaft drilled by Raine's great-great-great grandfather in his fruitless quest to discover gold a hundred years ago. "Here's the entrance at the foot of the White Gates, the one that I found when I ended up in that avalanche." He put his finger on the spot, his mind spinning back to the day when he was about to die, trapped at the foot of one of the avalanche chutes. He'd scrambled into the rocks and tried to find a place to hide from the avalanche, something deep and protected, and discovered one of the many entrances into Frederick Borsh's mine tunnels.

The tunnel saved him from the avalanche that day, and brought him to the surface a day later a long way away through a series of tunnels. Could he hope that Raine's great-great-great granddad connected his tunnels all over his mountain? He spanned the distance between the two X's with his hand and let out a breath. They were close enough that they just might be connected.

"You think there's a tunnel from here to there." Raine moved his hand and peered at the map. "We might find another way out."

"Maybe we can get out there. But it's risky. The tunnel could be collapsed already. Or there might not be enough air."

"I think you may have something here." Drake took the flashlight from Tor and aimed the beam back and forth between the two X's, the one where they were trapped and the one at the bottom of the White Gates. "Can you see those other marks on the map? The tiny ones? They're in between the two mine entrances."

"Those are super-small shafts. The most dangerous kind." Raine tapped the map. "The ones Roscoe helped us find this summer. Not big enough to fall into or anything, just enough to break your leg if you step into it. They're nothing but holes in the ground. Why would my great-great-great grandfather dig something like that?"

"Because they aren't holes," Drake said, and tapped one with his gloved finger. "They're air shafts."

Tor drew in a breath so deep he saw spots. "Air? Like—"

"Like for a tunnel." Raine put her gloves to her cheeks. "Tor, look at the mine entrance at the bottom of the White Gates. If those marks are air shafts, there's a tunnel from here right to it."

"Then let's get going." Tor held out a glove and Drake smacked it with his. Raine did too, and they grinned at each other.

"No need to bash Mr. Stanley's brains in," Drake said, as Raine folded up the map. He handed the flashlight back to Tor. "That's a relief."

"Oh, I'm still planning to bash his brains in." Raine put the map in her day pack and zipped it up. Her voice was as cold and clear as lake ice. "Mr. Stanley had better hope Sheriff Hartman gets to him before I do."

"He should." Tor aimed the flashlight down the tunnel at the green glow. "I guess we should get—"

"Tor." Drake snatched the flashlight away. He clicked it off.

"Hey—" Tor stopped. He could see a green glow, but it wasn't coming from deep inside the tunnel. The glow was outside the gate. Tor turned slowly and there at the entrance stood the ghost, his hat shadowing nothing, staring in at them from his eyeless face.

Time stopped as the ghost stared at them and they stared back, all of them still as statues, their breath curling into the air above their heads.

Wait a minute. The ghost's breath smoked around its head too. Ghosts didn't breathe. Tor's freezing hands turned into fists.

"Who are you?" He took a step forward, his anger washing away the fear in a flood. "What do you want?"

The ghost turned its head and looked back and forth, then dropped its hands from the gate and fiddled at something on its waist. A moment later the green glow flickered and disappeared. The ghost swept its hat from its head and tugged at something black. A covering came off and there, blinking at them, stood Pedro Martinez, the retired town handyman.

"What are you doing in there?" he asked.

Tor couldn't stop staring at the black mask hanging from old Mr. Martinez's hand, feeling so angry at himself his stomach felt sick. It was all a trick. The whole haunting was a trick. There was no ghost at all; the ghost was crazy Mr. Martinez playing some stupid game.

"You're the ghost?" Raine stepped forward to the chain-link gate. "Why?"

Mr. Martinez reached out with a hand covered in black gloves—that was why the ghost had no hands, it was all a trick, a stupid trick—and shook the metal gate. He tugged at the padlock. "You're trapped in here. Who trapped you in here?"

"Mr. Stanley did. Can you—" Drake started, but Mr. Martinez interrupted him.

"The toxic waste from the mine. It's back there?"

"Yes!" Raine rattled the metal gate with her gloves. "You knew about it?"

"I knew that slimy Stanley was doing something with it but I couldn't figure out what. He bought that new truck of his, and suddenly he's got all that fancy gear for skiing. I knew he got that money from somewheres. Then I picked up a rabbit one day out by my place that was all starved and dead and I knew where he was getting all that money. That's why I put you kids on the trail, to find out what was going on—"

"You put us on the trail?" Tor snatched his flashlight back from Drake and clicked it on. He pointed the light at old Mr. Martinez's face. The man winced and put up a hand, his face seamed with a thousand wrinkles.

"Aim that elsewhere, boy. I've been haunting the library for weeks trying to get you to figure out where the barrels were going. Didn't you look at the books? They were all about chemical dumps and contamination."

"Why didn't you just tell the sheriff?" Raine hammered at the gate between them, making the metal zing. "Why didn't you just tell someone?"

Mr. Martinez bowed his head, and they all fell silent. Tor didn't need him to explain. He already knew.

"They don't publish my letters in the newspaper no more," Mr. Martinez twisted his cowboy hat in his hands and then put it on his head. He stuffed his head covering into his pocket. He started shivering. "All I had was suspicions, like about them rays they're sending from the cable television that get into your brain. The tinfoil in my hat keeps it out. But nobody would listen to me. They didn't believe me about seeing Bigfoot, neither. I figured they'd listen to you."

Raine's gloved hands dropped from the metal fence as if she couldn't hold them up anymore. "So you haunted us instead."

"I knew you weren't understanding me with the books and stuff, but I didn't know what else to do," Mr. Martinez said.

"How did you escape through the basement shelves?" Tor asked. "You just disappeared."

"I took the books out from one of them shelves and put an empty paper bag there that I drew on so it looked like books," Mr. Martinez said. "I knew I might have to run from somebody so I had an escape plan. I always have one."

"You jumped through where the bag was taped onto the shelf and it looked like you were diving through the books." Drake shook his head in admiration. "We never guessed."

"It was kinda small for me and I rapped my head something fierce," Mr. Martinez said. "I heard the bookshelf go over. I was worried you got hurt but then I heard Tor's dog, Roscoe, so I grabbed the paper with the book drawings on it and got out of there. And you're all okay."

"We're fine, Mr. Martinez," Raine said. She sounded exhausted.

"Then when those government men said the poison was coming from this land, I knew that fool Stanley was storing it here, so at last I knew what he was doing with it. There's just a few mine openings on Borsh Mountain that could poison the water like that. Once I found that old road and seen it was plowed, I knew this had to be the place. So here I am."

"Now we all know. Can you get us out of here, now? Please?" Drake rattled the gate. "Mr. Stanley is going to come back here and kill us if we don't freeze to death first."

"Then we can all go to the sheriff and the mayor." Raine said. "They don't have to believe us about the toxins—we have the proof right behind us."

"I got my old truck down the ways a bit, it couldn't make it near as far as Stanley with his fancy plow on front. But we could walk to it and—" Mr. Martinez eyed the metal gate. "But first we have to get you out of here."

"Good idea," Tor said. His mom was going to be worried to death by now.

"I need a crowbar or something." Mr. Martinez shivered harder now. His old prospector's hat wasn't as warm as their snowboarding helmets. Tor kept his flashlight aimed at the snow instead of Mr. Martinez's face but the reflected light showed the old man's strained expression. "Stay right there, I've got to get back to my truck and get me some tools. And my winter hat. I wore my ghost stuff 'cause I was trying to scare Stanley away if he saw me. He hates spooks."

"Okay, Mr. Martinez. We'll wait," Drake said.

"Hurry," Tor said, and clenched his hands into fists. Then he heard something, a thudding, and realized it was the sound of running footsteps.

Mr. Stanley charged out of the darkness, his crowbar raised.

"No!" Raine shouted, but it was too late. Mr. Stanley swung his crowbar right at Mr. Martinez's head. The metal connected with a terrible hollow sound and the older man crumpled to the ground. None of them had seen Mr. Stanley coming. He turned to the three of them, panting hard, teeth glinting in the dim light of Tor's flashlight.

Drake crouched down to his backpack and snatched something out of it. He stepped forward and whipped his bike lock through the bars of the gate and pulled it tightly back. He clicked the lock shut before Mr. Stanley reached the gate, and they all stumbled back as Mr. Stanley hit the gate with his crowbar. The gate zinged and hummed and held.

"Gotcha," Drake said to Mr. Stanley.

Tor aimed his flashlight at Mr. Stanley's face. His eyes were wide and fixed, his mouth open and panting in the light. He looked like a person about to become a werewolf. He threw back his head and screamed and grabbed the fence and shook it again and again, then beat the crowbar across it. The chain rang and screamed too, but it didn't break.

"You can't do this!" he shouted. "You can't do this!"

"Time to go." Raine plucked at Tor's sleeve, stepping backwards. "Quickly."

"Mr. Martinez—" Tor bit his lip. They couldn't help the old man.

"I'll be back." Mr. Stanley struck the chain a final time and spun around. "You'll be sorry. You'll be sorry. There's nowhere to go. So you'll be sorry!" He disappeared into the dark.

Tor gave one more glance at the dark, still figure of Mr. Martinez in the snow and then turned and raced after Drake and Raine.

# Chapter Eighteen
## Through the Darkness

The glow sticks were faded and dim in the mine cavern, leaving smudges of green light and looming shadows everywhere. The barrels of toxic waste seemed larger than before, some packed closely together and some set at odd angles like tombstones in an old graveyard. The black hawk of Thayne Mining was everywhere on the barrels, the flashlight catching them and making them flutter. Now that Tor was closer he could see the spidery looking biohazard symbol plastered on the drums too.

"The map, Raine?" Tor made his voice calm. Raine dug it out and handed it to him without speaking, her lips drawn into an angry line. Dirt smudged her cheek.

"If these markings for air shafts are the same for all the mine entrances, there should be three tunnels out of here." Tor aimed his light at the map and forced his hand to stay still and stop trembling. "This is the one we need." He aimed his light at the far end of the cavern.

"We have to get by all those barrels." Drake took a deep breath. "Single file?"

"Single file," Raine said and took hold of the back of Tor's jacket. Drake grabbed the back of hers. Tor led, walking cautiously as though the barrels were filled with nitroglycerine. For all he knew they might be. Any of them might explode if he knocked into them. They were supposed to be taken care of, processed and recycled into something harmless. Instead they sat there, eating their way into the earth, into the ground, finding their way to water.

"Stupid man," Drake hissed, echoing Tor's thoughts.

"Yes." Raine said with a deadly calm. Tor stepped around a barrel and stopped, inhaling sharply.

"Go back." He gestured with one gloved arm. Raine peered over his shoulder. An inky lake of something covered the cavern floor in front of them.

"That is disgusting." Drake looked at the pool for a long moment and then backed up, allowing Tor to reverse his course. Tor found another path through the tumbled barrels, hoping another spill wouldn't block their way, hoping the tunnel would be open. His heart pounded so hard he could feel the heartbeat in his ears. His nose started to run and his eyes itched and stung in the bitter, acrid smell from the barrels.

His flashlight beam sank into the wall ahead of them and disappeared. He'd found an opening. This was their tunnel. Tor took a deep breath and led his best friends into the narrow crack, his flashlight making a cone of light in front of him. Any second a fall of rocks or dirt could block them and send them back to face Mr. Stanley, who had probably just murdered poor old Mr. Martinez and was not going to have any problems murdering them too. Or the mine could collapse on them, burying them forever underground. His friends depended on him to find the way out. Tor tried to breathe normally, tried to keep his flashlight from shaking in his hands, because Raine and Drake needed him and he couldn't let them down, couldn't let them see how he was so scared his legs barely worked.

Ahead of them the tunnel narrowed until it was barely wide enough for Tor's shoulders to fit through. Old timbers stood at intervals against the walls with cross bracing at the top to hold back the dirt. The timbers were made of pine, darkened with age. A fallen beam of wood loomed in the flashlight beam. Tor held his breath and stepped over it carefully, eyeing the ceiling. Raine stepped over too, her hand losing his jacket for a moment and then seizing his arm again.

"Ow, don't pinch me." Tor twitched and she loosened her grip.

"Sorry." Raine's voice was a bare whisper.

"It's okay." Tor nodded but he didn't look back. He aimed his flashlight up, seeking the air shaft that he hoped would be just ahead, the opening that would let fresh air down to them and keep them from suffocating.

They wouldn't suffocate. Tor kept telling himself that. Raine's great-great-great-grandfather Frederick Borsh never found the gold he wanted, but that didn't stop the old miner from making each tunnel level, straight, well aired, and braced.

Except that was more than a hundred years ago and the tunnels weren't going to last forever, no matter how sturdily they were built. The broken logs, the sagging ceilings, all were signs that these tunnels were going to collapse someday. The air shafts might already have closed, leaving them with poisoned air that would kill them. He'd done a lot of reading about mine shafts after he'd ended up in one two years ago. Mine shafts weren't just dangerous on the surface, where you could fall into them, or because you could be buried by falling rocks and timber. Mines collected bad air, like carbon dioxide. This gas was heavier than air, so it collected at the bottom of the tunnels.

Tor realized he was making a hissing sound through his teeth and stopped it. He kept walking, and then the beam of the flashlight lit a narrow crack that ran straight up into blackness. A thin stream of cold, fresh air struck his cheeks, and he closed his eyes and lifted his nose, smelling the snowflakes that must be falling outside right now. Raine crowded in close and so did Drake, lifting their faces greedily to the air.

"That's the first air shaft." Drake held up four fingers. "Four more."

"We're in the right tunnel." Raine nodded and made a *come on* gesture with her glove. "Let's move."

"I'm on it." Tor drew a last deep breath of the cold breeze and aimed his flashlight into the tunnel ahead. Raine took his sleeve and Drake clicked his flashlight on, just once, to check their back trail. Tor didn't think Mr. Stanley would creep up in the dark behind them, but Tor knew that Drake wasn't taking any chances. The tunnel was empty behind them so Drake clicked the light off again.

They walked along a long, clear stretch of tunnel and reached the next air shaft, which was big enough for a sifting of fine snow to make a little pile on the floor of the mine. The wood beams in the ceiling looked water soaked and sagged alarmingly, blackened with rot.

"Careful," Tor breathed, and tiptoed past the air shaft. He snatched breaths of fresh air as they passed the weakened area.

"Three airshafts left." Drake checked their back trail again. "Nobody behind us."

"We're going to get out of here." Raine smacked the back of Tor's coat, hard. "And we're going to get Mr. Stanley. Right, Tor?"

"Right." Tor bit back a nervous laugh. Raine was scary when she got mad, and she wasn't just mad right now. She was furious the way the gods in the Greek stories got angry, the ones that exploded volcanoes and turned people into stone.

"Next air shaft, up ahead. I am trying not to sound hopeful." Drake sounded hopeful. Tor aimed his flashlight up at the crack that drilled to the surface above them. This one seemed sealed up. No air flowed down to them. Tor frowned but said nothing, and they didn't pause.

"Two more, and we should be at the White Gates." Tor peered at the very limits of his flashlight beam, hoping to see moonlight, or a drift of snow. They had to be close.

"Great-great-great grandpa Fred knew how to build a tunnel." Raine let go of Tor's sleeve and slapped the back of his jacket again. "It's solid."

"Sure is." Drake laughed. "Solid as a rock."

Raine giggled.

Tor aimed his flashlight at the next airshaft. It, too, looked as if it had closed long ago.

"Last one." He squinted into the narrow cone of light. "We should be out soon."

"Soon, soon, all afternoon," Drake sang.

"You sing terrible, Drake." Raine giggled again. "I can sing better than that."

Tor took in a sharp breath. Horror flooded into him like icy water. They were breathing bad air. Raine and Drake were getting sick.

"Here's my song. I'm way better. A hunting we will go, a hunting we will go…"

"Hi ho a merry oh, a hunting we will go…" Drake joined her, and they laughed together.

"Hold onto me, Raine. Drake, hold onto Raine." Tor didn't feel the effects yet, but he knew he would soon. As Tor walked through the tunnel he stirred up the bad air, so Raine and Drake were breathing it in behind him.

He'd start feeling the effects soon anyway, even though he was in the front. They had to get out of the mine. Tor started walking faster, but then something looked different at the very edge of the flashlight beam. His heart sank as the tunnel split in two just ahead of them. One led left, the other led right. He didn't know which branch to take.

"A hunting we will go." Drake chuckled, his voice slurring.

Tor stopped and aimed his flashlight down one tunnel, then the other. Down the right tunnel, past the limits of the light, he though he saw something. It looked like a person, faintly glowing green, beckoning them on. It couldn't be the ghost. Mr. Martinez was the ghost and he was far behind them, in the snow, probably dead.

"Tor," Raine said. "I feel sick."

Tor grabbed Raine and yanked her forward into the right-hand tunnel, and Drake followed behind, breaking into a near run. The ghost, if it was a ghost, blinked out.

Tor gritted his teeth and ran on. He'd made his choice and there was no turning back.

"Tor, I'm tired," Raine complained, panting. "Let's rest."

"No!' Tor shouted, too loudly. Behind them he heard the sound he'd been dreading since they walked down the tunnel, a shifting and groaning as if something long dead was trying to claw its way out of the earth.

"Monsters!" Drake said, and laughed wildly. "Bring it on, monsters!"

"It's not monsters." Tor pulled them forward, not looking back, as the ground trembled and shook. A thump shook the earth, like a giant stomping down hard in the darkness behind them. Fine dirt swirled around them and shot forward as if it were running from the monster too, and Tor let his panic take him and they sprinted. Timber snapped and rocks crashed down behind them.

"Run, Tor!" Drake screamed.

Tor saw sparks and spots in front of his eyes and knew he was feeling the bad air too, that it was now a race between dying of poisoned air or dying under the crushing weight of tons of rock, and the spots were big, swirling, rotating like snowflakes, the snowflakes he loved to see falling through the air, the snowflakes that made his snowboard sing.

He staggered against the wall and nearly lost his footing. The flashlight jagged up and down in his hand and suddenly something huge loomed up in the light, an enormous thing as big as the tunnel. Tor didn't have time to flinch back when the creature seized his coat sleeve in its mouth and tugged hard.

Roscoe, his dog Roscoe, yanked him forward, and Tor was too dizzy to try and figure out how his dog was there. Roscoe's coat was full of wet snowflakes, and then the air was filled with them too as his dog pulled him out of the mineshaft and into the night.

"Come on!" Tor tried to scream, but it came out as a hoarse yell. He turned back to Raine and seized her coat, pulling her out into the open air. She stumbled forward and fell headlong. Behind them the crashing was continuous now, marching up behind them as the weakened timbers gave way one by one. Drake was ten feet behind, his eyes blinking and confused, his mouth slack, trying to run but tripping every step, catching himself on the wall, doggedly pushing himself forward.

Tor reached out but he was too dizzy, too slow, and Drake was staggering. Behind him, rocks and earth closed in, and Tor wasn't going to be able to reach him in time.

# Chapter Nineteen

## Nobody Trusts Anybody Around Here

A figure darted around him and into the tunnel, grabbed Drake's coat, and pulled him into a run. The two stumbled out of the entrance and fell into the snow. The tunnel crashed shut, sending a spray of rocks and dirt over Tor's boots and his legs. Dust billowed out and filled the air. The ground beneath them trembled and then quieted. They lay in heaps, panting, the cold snow feeling amazing on Tor's face. Every snowflake rubbed him happily like Roscoe rubbed against him when he got home from school.

Maybe that was the poisoned gas, Tor thought dizzily. Snowflakes aren't puppies. He looked up to see a tall cliff face in front of him. He knew where he was. The townspeople called these the White Gates, the two avalanche chutes visible from town. They were dangerous, steep cliffs of granite streaked with quartz, and no one snowboarded them even in the deepest snow.

Except Tor, that one time, and it wasn't on purpose and it had nearly killed him. He looked further up and wanted to see stars, but the sky was overcast, thick with clouds. Still, there were stars out there, up there, and he would see them soon. They were alive.

"Get off me, you waster." Drake's voice was muffled under the other figure.

"It's not me, Drake," Tor said.

The dark figure rolled off of Drake and even before Tor's flashlight lit her face he knew who it was.

"Who you calling a waster, townie?" Gemma said breathlessly, and grinned. She wore a black coat and snowboarding pants. A knit cap covered her pale blonde hair.

Drake sat up, holding his head. Raine scrambled to her hands and knees. They all regarded Gemma in Tor's flashlight beam. He aimed it away from her face so she wouldn't be blinded. Roscoe sat down next to Tor and nuzzled his face with his cold nose.

"How did you find us?" Drake asked.

"Roscoe found you. I've been checking every mine entrance on this side of Borsh Mountain since they closed the chairlifts." Gemma patted her coat front and pulled out a folded piece of paper. "Dad's on the Snow Park search and rescue team. He has a map for Borsh Mountain. It's super top secret. I'm not supposed to know about it. I knew you were going to be searching the mines when I tried to stop you at school today, Tor. I knew you were going to try and find the source of the poison. So I swiped the map."

"And my dog," Tor said. He put an arm around Roscoe and grinned at Gemma. "You rebel."

Gemma sniffed and put her map away, frowning at him. "Your mom was still at the clinic when I got Roscoe from your house. We've been searching for a long time. Roscoe took off at a gallop about twenty minutes ago. Good thing he was on a leash or I'd have lost him. I followed him. That's all."

"And you saved our lives," Raine said quietly. "Thank you." She stood up, staggering a little.

"Hey—" Tor said.

"Mr. Stanley—" Drake said at the exact same instant.

"Mr. Martinez!" Raine clutched at her helmet again. "Ow, my head. We have to get help. He might still be alive."

Tor couldn't see Drake's expression in the shadows of the flashlight, but he didn't need to. They'd both heard the terrible sound when Mr. Stanley hit the old handyman on the head.

"Mr. Martinez?" Gemma asked. "What's going on?"

"We'll tell you on the way." Tor scrambled to his feet. He felt as though his bones had turned to noodles, but he couldn't let that stop him. "We need to get back to town, fast."

"Roscoe and I followed an old road coming up here," Gemma said. "It looked like someone plowed it a few times. We can follow it back."

"Let's go," Raine said. "Quick as we can."

Gemma produced a flashlight, clicked a leash to Roscoe's collar, and started forward. Tor fell in next to her and explained about the mine and Mr. Stanley and what he'd done.

"That waster." Gemma hissed through her teeth. "All those poor animals, so sick and weak. He's evil."

"You got that right," Drake said from behind them. He sounded exhausted, and when Tor glanced back he could see his friend's face was pale. Raine, too, looked sick.

Gemma glanced back too, her eyes worried behind her glasses. Tor walked on the trail she and Roscoe had made but it was still tough going through the deep snow.

"Where do you think Mr. Stanley is now?" Gemma asked.

"We think he was going off to get explosives to seal the mine. I don't think he was going to let us out. I think he was going to seal us in," Tor said.

"Where was he going to get explosives?" Gemma asked.

Tor stopped in his tracks. "I never thought of that."

Behind him, Drake gave a shaky laugh. "Me neither. I just thought he knew how to get them or something."

"Handymen don't use explosives in their jobs," Gemma said, and nudged Tor to start him walking again. "And you can't just go buy them at the store. He could make them, I guess, but it would take a while."

"I didn't think about that," Tor mumbled.

"So maybe he was coming back with a gun," Raine said. "I can't think of any other way for him to get out of this other than killing us."

"Me neither," Drake said.

"But we got out. We have to get back and tell my mom," Tor said.

"And Grandmother." Raine said. "We will keep our land. I have to tell my family."

"But we have to watch out for Mr. Stanley when we get close to town," Drake warned. "If he's not at the mine, where is he?"

"Looking for us, I bet," Tor said. The snow dragged at Tor's tired legs as he took the lead from Gemma, giving her a chance to catch her breath. His flashlight beam lit the clear trail she and Roscoe had made. Around them, light snowflakes continued to fall.

"I can't believe I'm saying this, but I am so done with snow." Drake gave a tired laugh.

Tor laughed too and patted Roscoe, who trotted along side him. "No kidding." He kept his flashlight on the trail Gemma and Roscoe had made. A new, unhappy thought made his head hurt worse than all his bumps and bruises. "I thought Borsh Mountain was so dangerous that no one comes here, but now we find out there's an old road to the mine, and the search and rescue team has a map and everything. Who else has a map? Who else comes here?"

"I don't know," Gemma said. "But I don't think town people go here. It's marked 'No Trespassing' all along the roads, and everyone knows it's dangerous."

"Good," Drake muttered. Tor, thinking of the otters and their secret valley, nodded but didn't say anything in front of Gemma. They plodded on, Tor's legs feeling heavier and heavier with each step, and then he stopped and peered through the trees.

"Is that a fence?" he asked.

"I think it is." Gemma stepped up next to him. Roscoe wagged his tail happily. "I'd cheer but I'm too tired."

"That's the highway that leads into town." Drake puffed out a sigh of relief. "We made it."

Tor made his legs move once again. The sagging barbed wire fence with "Danger: No Trespassing" signs attached to it creaked slightly in the night. Tor stepped on one of the strands of wire, pushing it down so the others could go through. Then he did too, stumbling a little as he let the barbed wire go. Raine waded to the side of the road and stomped her feet in a circle, throwing out her arms.

Drake staggered onto the edge of the deserted highway and pulled Raine into a hug. "Almost home!" Tor got the same treatment, and so did Gemma, and for a moment the four of them stood in a circle, hugging, and Roscoe nudged his way into the center, his tail wagging. The solid footing felt great under Tor's boots, the first level ground he'd stood on since—when? The afternoon? The time fell on him like a weight. His mom would be frantic. So would Raine's folks.

"Let's get back fast." Tor stepped back. In his flashlight beam he could see Gemma looking rather pink and flustered. She busied herself with patting Roscoe.

Raine took out her cell phone and it lit up her face. She regarded it. "We have service now. Should we call home? What do we say?"

"Maybe we should do it in person?" Drake pointed his flashlight up and down the road. "We've got a lot of explaining to do—" He stopped and drew in a deep breath.

They all turned to look where he aimed his flashlight. The back of an old red truck stuck up from the ditch down the road. Red lights glowed like eyes.

"That's Mr. Martinez's truck!" Raine said. "What's it doing here?" She ran toward it and Tor followed, his aching legs complaining at every step. Roscoe bounded along with them. Tor and Raine waded into the deep snow that filled the ditch. Drake followed right behind them. Inside the cab, Tor could see the still form of Mr. Martinez lying against the steering wheel.

"Is he alive?" Raine dragged the door open. Warm air billowed out and hit Tor in the face, along with a smell of old guy aftershave and greasy tools.

"Careful, don't move him." Tor reached past Drake to put his fingers on Mr. Martinez's neck. He remembered the feel of the dead mountain lion, cold and hard and still, and gulped in a breath as his fingers touched warm, living skin instead. Mr. Martinez didn't move. His eyes were slightly open but it didn't look like he knew they were there. The side of his head was matted with dark blood.

"Mr. Martinez?" Raine put her hand on his shoulder but the old handyman didn't move. "Mr. Stanley must have dumped him here to make it look like Mr. Martinez was in an accident. We have to call the sheriff."

"He won't believe us, Raine." Drake shoved in next to Tor. He looked down on Mr. Martinez. "Let's go get your mom, Tor, so she can help him. I don't think we can get the car out of the ditch."

"You can drive?" Gemma asked.

"No, but I'd give it a shot," Drake said with a grin.

"And the sheriff?" Raine asked.

"He'll just blame us." Tor shrugged. "If he even believes us at all. That's probably why Mr. Stanley dumped Mr. Martinez here when he found out we were gone from the mine. He can pretend he didn't try to kill all of us and we don't have any proof that he did."

Gemma, on the roadway behind them, made a sound like an angry cat. They all turned. She put her hands on her hips and glared at them. "This whole time nobody trusted each other. I didn't trust you even though I knew there was something wrong with the animals in the woods. Mrs. Harbin didn't trust anyone enough to tell them about the ghost because she thought everyone would laugh and she'd lose her job. Mr. Martinez went through all this ghost business because he didn't trust the sheriff to believe him."

"And we didn't trust anyone but ourselves." Tor said slowly. "You're right."

"We don't need to trust anyone but ourselves," Drake said. "We never did. We never do."

Raine nodded, and Tor did too, more slowly. He glanced in the cab of Mr. Martinez's truck again, past the injured old man, and saw something on the seat. He started to grin. He turned around to his friends.

"I have an idea," he said.

"Oh, no," Drake said.

"What is it?" Raine asked.

"We're going to trust in the sheriff, and Raine's family, and Mrs. Harbin. We're going to trust Gemma. We're going to get help for Mr. Martinez. And then we're going to trust them to let us try something completely crazy."

"What?" Raine demanded.

Tor held up a black head covering he'd taken from Mr. Martinez's truck. "We're going to prove that Mr. Stanley tried to kill us. Raine, call your folks. Gemma, call your dad. Drake—call my mom. Then call the sheriff."

"The sheriff?" Drake wheezed. "Why me?"

"Because I don't have a cell phone, remember?" Tor said. Raine, Gemma and Drake rummaged in their pockets and soon the dim lights of three phones lit up in the darkness.

"What are we going to do?" Raine asked Tor.

"You know how freaked out Mr. Stanley was when he thought we saw a real ghost?" Tor grinned. "When he gets back to the mine and finds the gate is still locked and then he sees that the only other tunnel out of there is collapsed, he's going to think we're dead. So let's see what happens when the kids he killed start haunting *him*."

# Chapter Twenty

## The Library

"**M**rs. Harbin?" Mr. Stanley called out. "Mrs. Harbin? Where are you?" Tor watched from the shadows as the handyman pushed through the library entrance doors, limping. His hair hung over his forehead in untidy tufts. His nose was red and swollen from where Raine had bashed it with her snowboard helmet. He'd replaced his winter jacket with a clean new "Mr. Handyman Services" coat with the logo on the front pocket and his name in script above it, but his boots were soaked and left wet tracks on the polished wood floor.

A single light at the front desk made a pool of light. The rest of the library was dark.

"Mrs. Harbin? You said it was urgent—" Mr. Stanley blew out a frustrated breath and his voice grew louder. "It's been a long day—Mrs. Harbin?"

He clumped toward the desk, smoothing his hair down with his hand and attempting to put a cheerful smile on his face. He looked terrible. His eyes were bloodshot and sunken in his head, and his mouth twitched at one side like he couldn't control it. He'd been working and breathing in the fumes from the cave for days, and Tor wondered if his brains were eaten away by the chemicals.

"Hello?" His voice echoed and he jumped a little. "Hello?"

Tor nodded to Raine and Drake and took a deep breath. He pushed the button that turned on the green lights he wore under his clothes and glided out from the far end of the bookshelves.

Mr. Stanley froze. Tor hoped that he was seeing a boy-shape outlined in glowing green with no face underneath its battered snowboard helmet. Tor's black face covering felt suffocating, and the green light tape itched his skin like mad. Raine joined him, moving slowly like she was drifting. Drake stepped out too, glowing, his face hidden like theirs.

They stood silently. Mr. Stanley flinched backward and one leg buckled. He fell to the floor and scooted backward. Raine held up one arm and pointed at him.

"I didn't kill you!" Mr. Stanley screamed. "I didn't! I just left you there. You're the ones who went into the deep mine tunnels, I didn't do that. It isn't my fault you're dead."

Tor raised his arm and pointed at him, and then Drake did too. Mr. Stanley sobbed and scooted backwards some more.

"I wasn't going to kill you, and I didn't mean to kill Mr. Martinez. He shouldn't have found the barrels, and you shouldn't have either. If you'd just left everything alone I would have wrapped those barrels up so they'd stop leaking. You see? It's all your fault! It's all your fault so leave me alone!"

He covered his head with his arms and sobbed.

Tor, Drake, and Raine looked at each other and dropped their accusing arms. Tor took off his snowboard helmet and pulled the black covering from his face.

"That's good to know, Mr. Stanley," he said.

Drake pulled off his helmet and his face covering and so did Raine. The three of them walked down the corridor and stopped a dozen feet away from Mr. Stanley, who let his arms drop slowly as he stared at them from his bloodshot eyes.

"You—it's all a trick? This was a trick?"

"All a trick, and you fell for it." Raine clenched her fist around her black face covering as if she were closing her fist around Mr. Stanley's neck. "You just confessed to murder and polluting my family's land."

Mr. Stanley made one of his lightning changes. His face relaxed into smiling contempt and he scrambled to his feet. He brushed at his hair and straightened his jacket. "So what? I confessed to you kids? No one is going to believe you."

"Well, that's usually true." Tor grinned at him. "But we made a change."

"Change?" Mr. Stanley's grin faded a little.

"We decided to trust this time." Tor didn't look at Raine or Drake. He didn't need to. He knew they were smiling too.

"Sheriff?" Raine said quietly. "Can you please...?"

The lights clicked on, bright as searchlights, and out from the stacks of books stepped Sheriff Hartman. His hand rested casually on his holster and his eyes were shadowed by his hat, his mouth set in a stern line. Behind him stood Mrs. Harbin, her face pale, holding a cell phone in her hands and aiming it at Mr. Stanley.

"Greg Stanley, you're under arrest," Sheriff Hartman said. "For the attempted murder of Pedro Martinez, as a start."

"I didn't—I didn't—" Mr. Stanley backed up, his hands in the air, his face crumpling once again into that of a scared little kid. "I—it was all their fault!" He pointed at Tor, Drake, and Raine. "It was all them!"

Sheriff Hartman handcuffed Mr. Stanley with the ease of long practice, taking Mr. Stanley's pointing finger down and securing his hands behind him. The sheriff nodded at Tor and his friends. He didn't smile.

"Kids, you can head on home. We'll be along tomorrow for some more questions."

"Thanks, Sheriff." Tor couldn't stop grinning. The cords of green LED lights wrapped under his clothes were hot and sticky. They itched like crazy and he couldn't wait to tear them off, and he was so hungry he could eat every single thing in his mom's house, and he wanted to see Roscoe again and rub his head, and everything fizzed inside him like a million points of light.

"Home, Tor?" Drake asked. Raine grinned at them as if she, too, bubbled inside with stars and comets.

"Home," Tor said. "We did it."

Later, when great wheels of pizza were all devoured down to the last scrap, when Gemma had fallen sound asleep curled up next to Roscoe with her head pillowed on her father's giant winter jacket, when Raine's family had collected their coats and hats and hugged everyone good-bye, Tor's eyes started slipping closed no matter how hard he tried to stay awake. He blinked and his mom was giving a quick hug to Gemma's dad, who carried his sleeping daughter wrapped in his enormous jacket, and when he blinked again the kitchen was empty except for him and his mom and Roscoe sleeping on his bed in the corner. She put a last few cups in the dishwasher and turned to him with a tired smile.

"Bedtime, Tor. Drake sacked out an hour ago."

"I didn't want to miss anything," Tor said, feeling as if his head were floating several feet above his body.

"You never do," his mom said. She ruffled his hair. "I'm so proud of you."

"Thanks, Mom." Tor got to his feet, thinking that maybe he would just lie down and sleep next to Roscoe.

"I just thought of something," his mom said, smiling. "We won't be haunted by that green ghost anymore. You can sleep all night." She kissed him on the cheek and gave him a gentle push towards his room.

Tor stepped into the bathroom and picked up his toothbrush, half asleep. Roscoe was already curled up on his bed and Drake was sacked out in the upper bunk. He was nearly done when a thought struck him. The figure that beckoned them on inside the mine, the one that told them to take the right fork in the tunnel, that couldn't have been Mr.

Martinez. Who was it? What was it? He looked over at Roscoe and the lump that was Drake in the top bunk.

"Whatever it was, if it comes back, we'll handle it, too. Right, Roscoe?"

Roscoe didn't even lift his head. He just thumped his tail, twice.

# Epilogue

"Tor, wait!"

Tor stopped and turned around, to see Mr. Ewald trotting to catch up to him, his egg-shaped body looking more than ever like Humpty Dumpty in a white shirt and black pants. Around them, students streamed out the doors of Snow Park Middle/High School, everyone chattering in excitement, ready to begin the first day of summer break. The sun streamed through the windows and laid a beckoning path right to Tor's feet. He sighed.

"Yes, Mr. Ewald?"

"Thanks for waiting." Mr. Ewald stopped and panted for a moment, his bald head shining. "I wanted to ask you if you were willing to work out with the team this summer. You know, if you want to be an assistant team manager next year, you have to start now."

Tor blinked at Mr. Ewald, imagining what it would be like to be the smallest, youngest member of the snowboarding team, put there as a mascot to show the town that the bullies on the team were tamed now, that they wouldn't be cheaters anymore. He could see himself carrying water bottles and cleaning up towels. He could see David Malone tripping him, shoving him into lockers, and pretending it was all an accident, like the time he and his friend Max Nye almost got him killed in the White Gates.

All this happened in a blink. Tor smiled at Mr. Ewald and shook his head, back and forth, feeling sorry for the teacher. "No way, Mr. Ewald. No way. Gotta go."

"Tor, wait!" Mr. Ewald called again, but Tor was in the sunshine, out the doors of the school, free.

✳✳✳

Roscoe jumped up and down in the yard, waiting for Tor to open the gate so they could wrestle. Drake laughed, his sweater tucked into the straps of his backpack. He'd worn a sweater with a zombie Statue of Liberty on the front for the last day of school. The day was so warm they'd stripped down to their T-shirts on the walk home.

"Camping!" Drake dropped his backpack on the grass in the yard, and Tor threw his on top and patted Roscoe's wriggling body. Roscoe bounded to Drake and let the other boy pet him as Tor picked up a ball. Roscoe ran to get it when Tor threw it across the yard, his tail wagging.

"Fishing!" Raine called out, opening the gate. She wore shorts and a T-shirt. Her braided hair reflected blue-black highlights in the sunshine. "Hi, Roscoe!"

"Hiking, too. Your dad promised us we'd climb to the top of a mountain this summer. A fourteener, right?" Tor wrestled with Roscoe, pretending he was trying to get the ball away from him. Roscoe growled and shook his head, his tail wagging so hard his paws hopped up and down.

"Come in for a snack, kids. I have something to talk to you about." Tor's mom stood at the door, smiling, so Tor knew it couldn't be something bad.

"What's up, Doc?" Drake said. They trooped into the house and settled at the table after washing up, while Tor's mom busied herself setting out sandwiches and apple slices for them. She wore light blue clinic scrubs and her curly hair was held back in a ponytail. She usually wasn't home by now and Tor wondered what was going on. Roscoe lapped up water and then lay down next to Tor, putting his head on Tor's shoe.

"This isn't about Thayne Mining or anything, is it?" Raine asked.

"No." Tor's mom patted Raine's shoulder as she swept by. "They're so grateful that you kids uncovered the illegal dumping that I think they'd give you free water bottles for life. They'll be cleaning up Borsh Mountain for a while, but they'll get there."

"My family will make sure of it," Raine said, and bit an apple slice in half.

"Mr. Martinez is okay, right?" Tor asked. His mom nodded, enjoying their questions, her mouth still tucked in a smile.

"He's still in a rehab facility in Denver, but he's getting better. The brain injury would have been fatal if we hadn't gotten him to the hospital in time. He'll be grateful too, once he's recovered all the way."

"Maybe he'll offer us our very own tinfoil hats." Drake finished his sandwich and reached for the apple slices.

"Or some Bigfoot hair. That'd be excellent." Tor snatched away the last two apple slices before Drake could eat them all.

"You two," Raine sighed. "Okay, Thayne Mining is grateful, Mr. Martinez is okay, Mr. Stanley is awaiting trial, and my mountain is getting cleaned up. Right?"

"Right." Tor's mom leaned against the sink, still smiling.

"So?" They all said at once.

"So I've been offered a two-week medical seminar in a place called Tulum, Mexico. It's on the beach on the Caribbean."

Drake kept his smile on but it grew fixed, and Raine didn't bother to try. Her face fell.

"You're taking Tor with you?" she asked.

"Well, yes. But—I'm also taking you two."

There was a stunned silence.

"What?" Drake said.

"I've already spoken to your parents, Raine, and to your dad, Drake. It's only two weeks. You won't miss too much camping and fishing while you're on the beaches of Mexico."

Tor felt the beginnings of excitement in his belly. The beach? White sand beaches and ocean waves with his best friends?

"There's some places to explore, too. A ruined Mayan city called Coba is being excavated near there, and I'm hoping to get with the lead archeologist and have you accompany some of the team on their explorations."

Drake's mouth fell open. "A ruined Mayan city," he breathed.

"And the ocean." Raine clasped her hands together. "I've always wanted to see the ocean."

"We have to leave tomorrow, so you need to get home and get packed," Tor's mom said. "Your parents got a passport for you, Raine, and so did your dad, Drake. I wanted to keep it a secret until you got out of school today, so they did, too."

"Wow." Drake looked stunned. "I didn't know at all."

"What about Roscoe?" Tor looked down at his dog, who was sleeping peacefully with his head on Tor's foot.

"Your friend Gemma said she'd come over every day and take care of him. She told me she likes him best, anyway," Tor's mom said.

Tor exchanged grins with Drake and Raine. It still seemed odd to Tor that Gemma was their friend now, but she was. Still prickly as ever, but solid.

"I contracted with a temporary doctor to take over the clinic duties for two weeks. Our friend Argus Hayward will keep an eye on the house, too. Roscoe will miss you, Tor, but we'll be back before you know it."

"Okay. Okay!" Tor jumped up out of his chair. Drake stood up too, and Raine. They looked at each other, then they started high-fiving each other.

"This is going to be so fun!" Raine said.

"It's going to be epic." Tor laughed. "Unless Raine is kidnapped by a mysterious Mayan cult who believes that she's the reincarnation of a princess and we have to rescue her."

"I will rescue myself, thank you," Raine said, putting her chin in the air.

"But we'll show up to help. Does the jungle there have vines and stuff, like in the Tarzan stories?" Drake asked.

"I guess we'll find out," Tor's mom said. "I do know this: we're going on an adventure, and you're going to get in trouble somehow."

"It is what we do," Drake said modestly, putting his hands behind his back and scuffing at the floor with his sneaker.

"That's right." Tor bounced up and down on his toes. "So let's go!"

# The End

# About the Author

I was born in Los Angeles, California, where my grandparents lived, because my hometown didn't have a hospital. Central City, Colorado is an old gold mining town in the mountains. Central City didn't have television or radio reception and back then there was no Internet at all. My brothers and sisters and I spent our summer days reading books. We also explored the forests and old mining camps there.

When I was nine, my family moved to Cheyenne, Wyoming, where I discovered that the mysterious "radio" my aunt had given me as a birthday gift suddenly started playing music. I started writing stories at the same time my radio started playing music.

My novels for adults include the detective Eileen Reed mystery series *Ground Zero, Earthquake Games*, and *The Thirteenth Skull*. My middle grade novels include *The White Gates, Roscoe*, and *Haunted Waters*. *The White Gates* was a Junior Library Guild Premiere selection and a finalist for the Missouri Truman Award.

I'm a former chapter president of Mystery Writers of America and a member of Rocky Mountain Fiction Writers. I live in Erie, Colorado, with my family and I'm hard at work writing my next book. Visit my website for more information and fun: www.bonnieramthun.com. Thank you!

– Bonnie